Stephen Ames wan
stands between him a

The breeze ruffled Liz's bl
worked in the stream, and as it flowed down her back, her hair reminded Stephen of ripe wheat rippling in the field. *She is so beautiful. She is compassionate and loving toward everyone but me.*

As if she heard his thoughts, Liz looked up. Her eyes were the color of strong tea.

"Would you like some water to drink?" he asked.

Quickly looking down at her uneaten lunch, Liz shook her head.

"Liz, why do you avoid me? Have I done something wrong?" he asked softly.

Her blush sent a warm glow through him. Liz spoke so quietly, he had to lean toward her to hear her words.

"You are very kind to Edwina. I thank you for that."

"But why can't you and I be friends?" he insisted.

Stephen Ames thought he saw tears in her eyes before she turned away. He watched in amazement as Liz jumped up.

"I need to help my mother."

MARILOU H. FLINKMAN and her husband have retired to a home in Arizona. Since the Kairos Prison Ministry is not active in Arizona, Marilou has become a food bank volunteer. She says she has finally gotten out of prison, but the Lord has found another way for her to serve. She is active in her church in Chandler. The Flinkmans enjoy travel. They have been in the backcountry of Brazil, on safari in Kenya and Tanzania, and recently returned from Hong Kong. She is an avid reader, enjoys visiting the couple's six children and thirteen grandchildren, and likes fishing in Alaska. To find out how Marilou is currently involved, please visit her Web site at www.marilouflinkman.com

Books by Marilou H. Flinkman

HEARTSONG PRESENTS

HP258—The Alaskan Way

HP442—Vision of Hope

HP460—Sweet Spring

Summer Dream

Marilou H. Flinkman

Heartsong Presents

In memory of Beth

A note from the Author:
I love to hear from my readers! You may correspond with me by writing:

Marilou H. Flinkman
Author Relations
PO Box 719
Uhrichsville, OH 44683

ISBN 1-59310-044-2

SUMMER DREAM

Our mission is to publish and distribute inspirational products offering exceptional value and biblical encouragement to the masses.

All Scripture quotations are taken from the King James Version of the Bible.

PRINTED IN THE U.S.A.

one

Upstate New York, 1825

"I'm told the church board the new preacher is to live at my house," Meg declared, patting her dark brown coiffeur, although she never allowed a hair to be out of place.

Liz stared at her cousin in shock. Aunt Sally clattered her teacup in its saucer.

"You will do no such thing," the older lady stated firmly.

Liz looked from one woman to the other, wondering what would happen next. Meg had always gotten her way ever since her mother, Liz's aunt Beth, had died.

"It is not proper for you to have a single man living in your house. Does your father know about this?" Aunt Sally demanded.

Meg picked up her teacup. "Father won't care. Besides, he and my brother, Phillip, will be in the house, so why is it improper?" She looked disdainfully at Liz. "Your home isn't even a proper place for him to go for supper," she said with scorn.

"Pastor Ames will room and board with me," Aunt Sally stated. "Pastor Barnes called on me yesterday to say the elders have accepted my offer to have the new pastor live here." Liz's aunt calmly picked up the teapot and offered to refill the girls' cups.

Liz heaved a sigh and held her cup up for more tea. "My mother is the finest cook in upstate New York. Pastor Ames will be glad to visit our home for a meal, and we will be proud to have him," she said quietly.

"Humph." Meg refused the offered tea. "What will he think of your dim-witted sister?"

Tears filled Liz's eyes. "Edwina is not dim-witted. The pain she suffered when she was burned has left her a little slow." She bit her bottom lip to keep from saying something untoward. Having regained control of her thoughts, she said, "My sister is so sweet. Why do you talk about her like that?"

Ignoring her cousin's discomfort, Meg put her cup down and rose from her chair. "I have to be going. Mrs. Greely is coming to fit my new dress." She flounced out of the house.

"It breaks my heart when Meg talks like that about Edwina," Liz said, breaking the silence that followed the sound of the front door closing. She wiped tears from her cheeks.

"Meg is well named," Aunt Sally observed.

"My mother says that too. What does her name mean?"

"It's not what her name means. It's who she was named after: your maternal grandmother, who lived in Connecticut. Never did understand why your aunt Beth named her daughter for that woman. She was a deceitful person who almost cost your parents their marriage." Aunt Sally took a sip of her tea.

Liz looked into her cup. "I wish Meg would get to know Edie." She smiled. "Numbers are hard for her, but she can read the Bible now."

"You've done a good job teaching your sister. What will happen when you get the schoolmistress job?"

"Oh, Aunt Sally, you are far more confident in my ability than I am. If I do get the job, I will live at home so I can continue to teach Edie."

"I had planned to have you live here, but the new pastor needed a place to stay. I hope you aren't upset."

"We aren't that far out of town. I'll ride to school. I might have to leave my horse in your barn if it would be all right."

"There's room for your horse, and I suppose Pastor Ames will have one too. What about the snow in winter?"

"I could take the sleigh, but if I can't get to the schoolhouse, the children won't be able to get there either. It'll work out." She put her cup and saucer on the table next to her chair. "Do you think I'll get the job? Meg seems to believe that because she is twenty and I am only nineteen she should have it."

"How did the interview with the school commissioners go?"

"It seemed to go well. Mr. Howard still wants to consolidate all the school districts in this area. That will be the end of the small schools throughout the town. He even wants the new school building to be big enough to hold a high school."

"That won't be finished for awhile. Originally Mr. Howard wanted the new school built in 1824, and it's already a year late. Will you get the Post Number Six School?"

"If I get to teach, that will be the school. It's also where Pastor Ames will hold church on Sundays."

Aunt Sally shook her head. "I don't know where it will end with Meg. She has scorned every eligible bachelor around here, but I guarantee she will be after this new preacher." She reached to pat Liz's hand. "That is why I went to see Pastor Barnes. He liked the idea of having Pastor Ames live here."

"So you can protect him from my cousin?" Liz asked shyly.

"It may come to that," the older lady said sadly. "Now tell me about your family. Your mother hasn't been to town for two weeks."

"Mother is busy with her spring housecleaning."

"You could eat off her floors. Why does she have to clean?"

Liz laughed. "You know my mother. It's spring and time to clear out the winter dust and dirt. I need to get home and help her." She crossed over to Aunt Sally and planted a kiss on the still-firm cheek. Years earlier, as a young widow with two small children, Sally Davis had married Liz's grandfather. The family loved the woman and called her Aunt Sally as a sign of respect. "Are you sure you aren't going to set your cap for the new pastor?"

"I have been widowed twice. No reason to think I should want to go through that again. Besides, Pastor Barnes tells me this Stephen Ames is young and good-looking." She reached up to pat Liz's cheek. "He might be the one for you."

Liz sputtered. "I don't have time for a beau. I just hope I get to teach the children. Now I'm off to get the things Mama sent me for. Do you need anything? I could drop them off on my way home," she offered.

"Thank you, Child, but I can still make it to the mercantile. I like to get out for a walk now that the snow is gone."

❧

A short while later, Liz entered her uncle David's store. "Hello, Phillip," she said, in greeting Meg's older brother. "Are you working hard?"

"Harder than my sister," he said. "But that wouldn't take much. Your mother and Aunt Sally have tried to teach her to sew and cook and keep house, but now she has to have a seamstress and a hired girl to cook and clean."

Liz frowned. "She'll find her place soon enough."

Phillip leaned on the counter and laughed. "I hear she has decided to be the new preacher's wife."

"Then she'd better learn to cook and sew. A preacher can't afford a maid," Liz retorted. She clapped her hand over her mouth, appalled. "Why do I always criticize that girl? She's had a hard life."

Phillip looked pained. "I lost my mother too. And you have lived with Edie's pain and suffering. Why should Meg get all the attention?"

"I don't know, Phillip. But I do know God calls us to be compassionate, and I must try harder." Liz pulled a list out of her pocket. "Now, I need some things for Mother."

The two cousins gathered the items on the list, and then Phillip tied the purchases into a small bundle. As she waited, Liz asked, "Where is your father?"

"Been out tapping the maple trees. He still likes to work outside when he can get away from running this store and serving as town supervisor."

"I'm not sure what Father and Matthew are doing today. I think they were going to work in the orchard. Maybe Uncle David is going to help them."

Phillip shrugged. "He knows I like to keep the store going, so he's free to do what he wants."

"And how is the blacksmith's daughter?" Liz's voice held a hint of mischief. She grinned at the blush her words brought to her cousin's face.

"Miss Whitney has invited me to supper tonight," Phillip admitted with a proud smile.

"Tell her hello for me." Liz gave him a mischievous smile and waved as she left the mercantile.

❧

"You must have stopped to see your aunt Sally," Mother said when Liz came in the front door of their farmhouse that afternoon.

"She sends her love." Putting her bundle on the table, Liz added, "She's taking in the new pastor as a boarder."

Her mother stopped stirring the contents of the pot on the stove and looked at Liz. "Whatever for?"

"Meg wanted him to live at their house, but the elders accepted Aunt Sally's offer of her home instead," Liz explained.

"A wise decision. We'll meet the new pastor on Sunday and see if he really needs Sally as a guardian."

"Did you bring me a present?" a voice called from the parlor.

"Did you do your lessons?" Liz answered, opening the bundle and taking out a small bag of hard candy.

Her dark-haired sister, Edwina, limped into the kitchen, holding a Bible. *She looks so like Mother,* Liz thought for the hundredth time. She took the Bible from her sister's hand.

"I read all the pages you told me. You want me to read them to you?"

Liz hugged her sister. She had been ten when Edie, then age six, had been burned. She had watched her mother's hair turn white almost overnight, caring for the tormented child. A special tenderness filled Liz whenever she saw her sister—and a wish that she could somehow have prevented the accident. "Let me hang up my cloak, and we'll read together." Turning to her mother, she asked, "Do you need help?"

"I have a pot of soup going. You girls can set the table when you're finished with the lesson."

As she sat down next to Edie to hear her sister read, Liz thought over the conversations she'd had during the afternoon. *I wonder,* she thought, *exactly what kind of man this new preacher will turn out to be.*

❧

Liz's family climbed into the wagon on Sunday morning for the ride in to the Post Six schoolhouse. As they approached the wooden building, Liz looked at the school and prayed she would get to be teacher there. Thoughts of teaching temporarily drove away her curiosity about the new pastor.

Liz's father had the horses pull the wagon up beside some other vehicles, and the family got down and made their way into the building. As they entered, Liz took Edwina's hand and gave her a reassuring squeeze. Her sister was usually nervous in public and self-conscious about her limp.

"Good morning and welcome," a deep voice spoke in greeting.

Liz looked up from guiding her sister. She stared into the darkest eyes she had ever seen. Liz forgot to breathe as she studied the stranger, who was certain to be the new preacher. His long hair, the color of a blackbird's wing, had been tied at the nape of his neck with a black band. Absently, she reached to pat her own honey blond tresses to see if they had escaped the bun on the back of her head. She couldn't speak. When her father introduced the family, she simply nodded at Pastor Ames politely, still stunned by the new emotions he stirred within her and hoping desperately that he wouldn't notice her silence.

two

Liz followed Edie and her mother to the front of the room. She motioned for her sister and mother to sit on the child-sized chairs while she stood with her father and brother to the side. Sternly reminding herself that she was here to worship, not daydream about the new preacher, Liz tried to rein in her galloping emotions.

A commotion at the back of the building drew everyone's attention. Liz turned and saw her cousin Meg making her way through the crowd with her head held high. Meg pushed her way to the front and center of the hall. Glaring at Aunt Sally, the young woman sat down next to her older relative. As Meg spread out her full skirt and petticoats, Matthew poked Liz in the ribs.

"Doesn't want to muss up her dress," he whispered.

Liz stifled a smile at Aunt Sally's frown and her attempts to push Meg back to her own part of the space they shared.

Just then, Pastor Barnes walked to the front of the room. Standing in front of the teacher's desk, he called for attention. "I started here years ago when we were meeting in homes," he recalled. "Then my son-in-law came to help out. When he and my daughter took over the church in Colosse, I became your pastor again. Now it is time for me to retire. We are blessed with a wonderful man for a replacement." Pastor Barnes motioned Pastor Ames forward. Putting his arm around the younger man's shoulders, he continued, "You will be well cared for by Pastor Stephen Ames."

Liz looked at the man standing next to Pastor Barnes. *Pastors aren't supposed to be young and handsome,* her mind protested. When Pastor Ames led the congregation in prayer, Liz had trouble hearing the words over the pounding of her heart. His voice carried her feelings to a place they had never been before. She held her breath, sure that her brother would hear her heart beat.

The congregation stood to sing a hymn. Liz took hold of the book Matthew offered to share. She did not answer his puzzled look when she didn't join in the song. *This has got to stop. What is wrong with me?*

As the service continued, she focused on the corner behind Pastor Ames, trying to avoid the unsettling feelings she experienced every time his dark eyes met hers. His deep, rich voice filled the room as he read from the Bible and preached to his flock about the love of God.

Matthew nudged Liz and nodded his head toward Meg. Irritated to be interrupted, Liz impatiently glanced at her cousin. Meg posed with a rapt look on her face for the new preacher. She had seated herself directly in front of him. Involuntarily, Liz shuddered, realizing that Aunt Sally's suspicions about Liz being after the new preacher appeared to be well founded.

Looking around the room after the last song had been sung, Liz saw by the smiles and nods that the congregation felt the pastor had a strong faith and would be a good leader. Her mother rose from her seat and took Liz's arm. "I want to speak to Alice Greely."

Nodding with understanding, Liz took her sister's hand. "Let's follow Matthew to the door," she told Edie. "He's big enough to make a path for us in this crowd."

"The preacher's handsome," Edie whispered.

"Meg thinks so," Matthew said with a grin.

"You should not speak ill of our cousin," Liz admonished her brother. The three siblings stood quietly while their mother waited for Mrs. Greely to make her way to the door.

"Why, Alice, you look peaked. Are you feeling ill?" Mama's voice held concern.

Alice shook her head just as Phillip joined his cousins.

"Poor lady is tired," Phillip growled. "Meg kept her up all night finishing that dress." He motioned toward his sister.

Mrs. Greely's lips curved upward, but her smile held no warmth.

"She wanted to wear it today," the seamstress said quietly.

The group turned to see Meg simpering in front of Pastor Ames. He looked uncomfortable to have her blocking the way of others seeking to speak to him.

"Let's go," Phillip said to Matthew. The two young men made their way to the pastor.

❧

Stephen Ames relaxed as two young men approached Miss Margaret on either side, put their hands under her elbows, and whisked her away. On his first Sunday with this congregation, Stephen wanted an opportunity to meet everyone, and he had been concerned Miss Margaret would monopolize his time. Freed from her attentions, he worked his way around to those whom he had not yet greeted.

He tried to make his way to the lovely young woman standing by the back door. He remembered how her face had brightened when her father introduced them before church. He'd noticed her standing quietly with her brother and father during the service. Now he admired the way she looked after the younger girl with her. He knew he wanted to get to know this young woman better.

Several ladies surrounded him, offering to have him come to dinner. He looked up from the group busy setting times and days for him to share their hospitality and saw the two girls leave the building. For some reason, he felt a twinge of disappointment that he hadn't been able to speak to her.

❧

On the wagon trip back to their farm, Liz's father told his family that several of the men he spoke to that morning had suggested building a church. "That school building is small and uncomfortable."

"But Liz is going to teach there," Edie protested.

"We hope so," Father said, looking at his youngest daughter. "What I meant was the building is designed for children. It's not the best place to hold church with all the adults."

"Where would you build?" Matthew asked.

"Your uncle David said he would look for an appropriate lot and see what it would cost. He even suggested we might be able to work to earn the land."

"I could help," Matthew offered.

"That was my brother's idea. There are men who couldn't give money but could donate labor to help get a church built." Liz's father looked over at her mother, who sat beside him. "I invited the new pastor for supper on Wednesday. I didn't think you would mind."

"That will be nice. I'm sure Sally will have lots of people wanting to feed her boarder."

"Like Meg," Matthew said, chuckling.

"She can't cook," Edie objected. "You said so yourself." She giggled and gave her big brother a friendly jab.

"She has a maid who will do it for her," Liz explained. "Meg doesn't have family to help her."

"Why doesn't Mama have a maid?" the girl asked Liz innocently.

"She has us. Families help each other—it's the Lord's way."

"I'm glad," Edie said, reaching over to hug her sister as the wagon pulled up by the farmhouse. "You help me read and do lessons."

Matthew and Father soon had the wagon and horses taken care of and walked into the kitchen where Liz's mother was putting last-minute touches on the meal she had left on the back of the stove to heat while they were in church. The family gathered around the table, said grace, and soon was enjoying the delicious food.

"Are the apple trees starting to bud?" Liz's mother asked near the end of the meal.

"I don't know," Father replied. "It's a nice day. Why don't we walk out together and look," he suggested.

"You go," Liz urged her parents. "Edie and I will wash up the dishes."

"Then will you read to me?" Edie asked.

"You dry the dishes and put them away for me, and I'll read to you."

But as she dipped the dirty dishes into hot, soapy water, Liz's thoughts continued to return to Pastor Ames and the disturbing feelings he stirred up in her. Liz gave herself a mental shake. Her priorities were helping care for Edie and, if the Lord so willed, to start teaching in the schoolhouse. She didn't have time to stand around mooning over a man—no matter how intriguing he might be.

❧

As Wednesday approached, Liz found herself worrying about spending an evening in such close proximity to Pastor Ames. No matter what her intentions were about focusing on Edie and teaching; based on Sunday's experience, she feared she would do something to betray her confusing feelings. And it would simply be too embarrassing to have the new pastor think she was enamored with him.

"Are you worried about the teacher's job?" Liz's mother asked as they prepared supper on Wednesday afternoon. "You seem so quiet and distracted."

Liz nodded, not wanting to admit that she had more things on her mind than just the board's decision about hiring a teacher.

"Don't be concerned," her mother said encouragingly. "The Lord will show you the right way."

"I know," Liz said. "And I continue to pray about it. But sometimes it's hard to wait."

As her mother gave her a warm hug, both women heard the sound of a horse coming up the drive. Liz gulped. Pastor Ames must have arrived.

Liz and her mother went out the front door and found Pastor Ames greeting the family warmly.

"Did you have trouble finding us?" Liz's father asked as he led the pastor's horse to the barn.

"Sally Miller told me how you brought the first apple seedlings in your saddlebags years ago, so I just looked for the hills covered with apple trees and knew I had come to the right place."

When they entered the house, the pastor stopped to take Edie's hand. "And who is this young lady? I saw you on Sunday, but I don't think we had an opportunity to be introduced. I would never forget the name that belongs to a face as pretty as yours."

Edie blushed and looked at her mother, who quickly intervened. "This is Edwina, our youngest daughter." Liz's mother moved closer to put a comforting hand on her daughter's shoulder.

"Sally Miller told me you had two daughters. I'm glad to meet you, Edwina," Pastor Ames said, releasing her hand.

Liz felt a warm glow when she saw the pleasure in her sister's face. Edie shied away from people. They tended to ignore her because of her crippled body.

"Will you be my friend?" Pastor Ames asked.

"Oh, yes," came the excited reply.

Following the pastor's lead, Father asked Edie to say the blessing before their meal.

"And please, God, bless my new friend," the girl said at the end of her prayer.

Liz blinked back tears that flooded her eyes. It wasn't often that a man showed such genuine interest in Edwina and in such a compassionate way.

The meal had a festive air, and as he piled another helping of pot roast on his plate, Pastor Ames observed, "Sally told me you were the best cook in the township, Mrs. Miller. Now I believe her."

Liz's mother smiled at the compliment. "Sally had to teach me to cook when I came to the frontier."

"Then I'll tell her she's a good teacher," Pastor Ames said with a smile.

While the women cleared the table, the men sat over coffee cups talking about the area. "We have a gristmill, tanneries, and shoe shops. We have clothing works, an ashery, a blacksmith, even a post office in Millersville," Liz heard her father tell the pastor. "What we need is a church building."

"The school is small," Pastor Ames admitted, taking a sip of coffee, "but where would we build?"

"George Scriba holds a Dutch patent on this land from before we became a country. This area was still owned by the Dutch when he purchased it. Most of us have bought our land from him. My brother David is going to contact him about what lots are available and what our cost would be."

"Does Mr. Scriba live around here? I could go call on him."

"No, he lives in Rotterdam, but he has a land agent in Oswego. David often goes there for business and offered to start negotiations."

"Let me know what I can do to help. I know how to pound a nail, so I can definitely lend a hand in the building process."

Just then at her mother's urging, Liz took the coffeepot to the table and offered refills. Pastor Ames held up his cup, but she was grateful he didn't seem to notice how the pot shook as she poured his coffee.

"Thank you, Miss Elizabeth," he said.

Liz avoided meeting his gaze and instead simply nodded and quickly turned back to the big iron cookstove. What was happening to her that she couldn't perform as simple a task as filling a cup of coffee without being overwhelmed by nervousness?

"Liz is worried about getting a job," her father said in what Liz recognized was an attempt to explain her shyness. "She hopes to be the schoolmistress in the school where the church meets."

"Oh," Pastor Ames said, surprise coloring his tone. "Miss Margaret told me she had the job."

Father shook his head. "Both Meg and Liz have applied for the job, but the commissioners have not yet named a new teacher. Of course they would prefer a man, but none applied for the position. We will have to wait to see which girl is selected."

"Well, Miss Elizabeth, we will pray the best candidate becomes the new teacher," Pastor said, putting his cup down.

"Liz is my teacher," Edie chimed in. "I can read the Bible."

The pastor smiled at Edie, and Liz wondered at his ability to put her younger sister at ease so quickly. The girl rarely spoke to anyone other than Aunt Sally outside the immediate family. But here she was volunteering information to the new pastor.

Pastor Ames turned to the girl. "I knew we would be friends, Edwina. I'll come again when we have time for you to read to me." He reached out to take a cookie from the plate Edie offered him. "Did you help your mama bake these?"

"Yes." Edie beamed.

And as the evening drew to a close, Liz only wondered why she couldn't feel as comfortable around Pastor Ames as the rest of her family did. Something was definitely wrong with her, and she needed to find out what it was before it created real problems.

three

Another meal out, Stephen thought a few evenings later as he left Sally Miller's house and started to walk to the other end of town. *I hope David Miller has invited me to talk about a new church building. Oh, Lord, guide me to know Your will.*

"Wait a moment, Pastor."

Stephen turned to see Phillip Miller locking the door of the mercantile. "Nice to see you, Phillip," Pastor Ames said, stopping to greet the young man.

"I'm on my way home, and I thought we might as well walk together."

"When did your father get back from Oswego?" Stephen asked.

"Oh, he'll not be back for another day or two. He's usually gone several days when he makes a business trip."

"But I—"

"Thought that is why you were invited for dinner?"

"Yes," Stephen stammered. "Your sister came by yesterday to extend the invitation."

"Aunt Sally told me about it. That's why I closed early tonight. I didn't want my sister to embarrass you."

"I'm confused. Are you saying this is your sister's doing?"

Just then a middle-aged woman walked toward them. Both men stepped aside to let her pass.

"Hello, Mattie," Phillip said. "How are you this evening?"

"Fine, Mr. Phillip. Miss Margaret sent me home early tonight, but I left your favorite fish dish cooking. It'll be ready for your dinner when you get home."

"Have you met our new pastor?"

Stephen tipped his hat to the woman. "Last Sunday in church. Nice to see you again."

"You have a good evening, Mattie. Pastor and I are going to enjoy the meal you cooked for us."

Continuing on their way, Phillip explained, "Mattie has been our maid since Mother died. She's a good cook."

"Nice of your sister to let her go home early."

"Hmmm, I wonder why?" Phillip said no more but opened the front door of his home for the pastor.

Meg came rushing to the door. Stephen stopped, stunned at the look she gave her brother. "What are you doing here?" she demanded of the young man.

"I came to join you and Pastor Ames for dinner," he said calmly.

Stephen looked from one to the other. Could she have planned to entertain him alone?

Meg turned to him all smiles and offered to take his hat. "Come right in. Dinner is ready."

He noticed that she quickly set another place at the table. He chatted with Phillip about the town as Meg brought bowls and platters to the table. When Stephen said the blessing, he silently added a prayer for guidance. *This woman could be trouble, Lord. I need Your help.*

"The fish is delicious, Miss Margaret," Stephen said a few minutes later.

"I'll give Aunt Sally the recipe so she can prepare it for you."

"Nice of you to let Mattie go home early. We saw her on our way here," Phillip said.

Again Stephen noticed Meg glower at her brother.

Stephen struggled with the awkward situation. The food he ate formed a lump in his stomach. After dessert, the men moved to the parlor for coffee while Meg carried the dishes to the kitchen. Soon after Meg rejoined them, Stephen rose. "I appreciate your having me to dinner," he told his hostess. "And I know how busy you are, Phillip, so I really thank you for closing early and joining us this evening. I am sorry your father did not make it back in time to be here. I'm eager to hear about his business trip to Oswego."

Making his way home in the cool spring evening, Stephen pondered the problem of Meg. *Dear Lord, I need Your help. How can I turn this young woman to Your ways and at the same time avoid the appearance of evil? I place this situation in Your hands and trust You to guide me.*

❧

When Liz dropped by to visit Aunt Sally the next afternoon, the older lady insisted on making a pot of tea. "Pastor Ames is going out to dinner again tonight. I don't think he has been here for more than breakfast since he moved in," she fussed as she poured a cup for Liz.

"He would never miss your cinnamon rolls for breakfast," Liz replied.

"Mattie came by earlier. She asked for my recipe. She'll be making them for David and Phillip." Sally passed the plate of cinnamon rolls. "And I'm sure Meg will have some on hand when the pastor comes to call. Pastor Ames told me he enjoyed dinner with Meg and her brother last evening," Aunt Sally added. "I don't understand why Meg didn't wait until her father could be there."

"Perhaps she thought her father would be back with news about land for the church," Liz said softly.

"Hello there," said a deep voice Liz immediately recognized. "I came to freshen up before going to the Wheelers'."

Liz felt as if a dozen butterflies were fluttering around in her stomach.

"Would you like a cup of tea?" Aunt Sally offered.

"Yes, thank you, and how nice to see you, Miss Elizabeth." The pastor's voice held a note of warmth that sent a blush to her cheeks.

"How do you do, Pastor Ames?" Liz whispered.

Pastor looked away from Liz long enough to take the cup Aunt Sally held out. "I have been hoping to see you again," he said, sitting in the chair closest to Liz.

Liz's mouth went dry. "Thank you for being so kind to my sister. She is really taken by you."

"May I ask you about her?"

Liz looked into her teacup, reluctant to refuse him his request but hesitant to relive that painful time in her family's life.

"Tell him, Liz," Aunt Sally urged. "It will be easier for you than for your parents to have to explain."

Closing her eyes, Liz could see the accident as if it were yesterday. Quietly, she spoke the words to describe what she saw. "The day was bitter cold. Edwina was playing with her doll by the fireplace. She dropped the doll and moved to pick it up. Her skirt flipped into the fire."

Anguish filled Liz's voice. "I saw the flames catch on the material and sweep across her little body. I screamed." She looked up, pleading with the pastor to understand her hurt.

"I should have kept better watch over her. She should not have been that close to the fire."

Sighing deeply, Liz went on. "Mama grabbed the bucket of water on the shelf and threw it over Edie. I pulled her away from the fireplace." Liz paused to catch her breath. "Edie didn't cry at first. It was as if time were suspended. Then she began to scream in torment, and I thought her cries would never end."

Looking up, Liz felt the tears drip on her folded hands. "My beautiful little sister was only six years old. I ran to draw more water from the well while Mama tried to pull the scorched cloth away from Edie's body. Her screams will haunt me the rest of my life. Mama poured more cold water over the burns while Edie's right side bubbled in huge blisters."

The pastor moved closer to Liz and took her hand. "How old were you?"

Liz looked into his nearly black eyes that melted with kindness. "Ten."

"It's a miracle that Edwina lived through it," Aunt Sally said. "She suffered unbelievable pain."

Liz looked to the old lady. "Aunt Sally came to stay with us. Mostly she was there to comfort my mother. Mama would hold Edie's hands and sing to her for hours. Edie had reached away from the fire so her hands didn't get burned, but her legs were charred. She couldn't stand anything to touch the burns. My father built a wooden frame to hold the quilts off her body."

"Did you have a doctor?" Pastor asked.

Liz nodded. "Granny Wheeler sent one of her sons to fetch the nearest doctor."

"Polly Wheeler is the midwife here," Aunt Sally explained. "She was one of the first settlers in the area and learned a little medicine from the Indians."

"I don't think the doctor expected Edie to live," Liz recalled, continuing her story. "He gave her laudanum to ease the pain. Polly told Mama to keep the wounds clean and open to the air. Father didn't like to have Edie take the laudanum, but he did let Polly give the child herbs to ease her pain." She looked into Pastor Ames's face. "Mama's hair turned white. She suffered right along with Edie."

"That was only part of her suffering," Aunt Sally told the pastor. "When Emily and her sister, Beth, came out to this country years ago, Phillip was only a few months old. Beth told me she and the baby slept in the sled one night, but Emily stayed awake. She saw her brother in-law and the man with them use flaming branches to fight off a pack of wolves. To this day Emily fears wolves."

The pastor sat back in his chair. "What have wolves to do with this?" he asked in a puzzled tone.

"My father needed money to build a house with stoves instead of fireplaces. He grieved over what had happened to Edie and wanted the fireplace out of our lives." Liz sniffed and pulled a handkerchief out of her pocket. "There was a bounty on wolf hides, so he hunted them to earn money to build us a new home."

"Another time, Jonathan and David hunted wolves and used the bounty to pay off their land," Aunt Sally told the pastor. "Back then the bounty was ten dollars. When Edwina was burned, the bounty had gone up to thirty dollars a hide, and nothing Emily could say would keep Jonathan from hunting them." She reached to touch Liz, whose tears continued to fall. "Liz is right. Between the accident and having Jonathan gone, hunting wolves, Emily carried tremendous burdens, and her hair turned white almost overnight."

"My father built the house where we live now," Liz explained. "We have stoves but no fireplace. Father tore down the cabin. He could not stand to see the place where Edie was hurt."

❧

Stephen desperately wanted to comfort this sweet young woman who cared so lovingly for her younger sister, but he knew he needed to understand the entire story. "The pain is what slowed Edwina's mind?" he asked gently.

"The shock of the fire robbed her mind," Liz answered. "She had started to read and write before the accident. Afterward, she had to start again. It was as if her mind refused to go back to the awful time of pain and suffering." With her head bowed, Liz whispered, "I did not save her from the fire, but I have tried to take care of her since that awful day."

"I am sure you did all you could to save your sister," Stephen said softly while thinking, *And I fear you will give up too much of your own life continuing to protect her.*

"We told Liz she could not have prevented what happened, but she still blamed herself," Aunt Sally said.

Stephen Ames put his hand over Liz's. "What a terrible tragedy for you and your family to live through. You gave up your childhood the day it happened." His heart ached to ease the burden Liz carried.

"God brought us through," she whispered.

Stephen patted her hand. "The book of Romans tells us, 'Now the God of hope fill you with all joy and peace in believing, that ye may abound in hope, through the power of the Holy Ghost.' " He gazed steadily into her tear-filled eyes. "I pray you will know that joy and be able to trust Him with the future."

Liz looked at him in confusion, and he offered a sympathetic smile. He understood that once a person had lived with tragedy for years, it could be hard to embrace life with enthusiasm. Yet maybe these words of Scripture would encourage this brave young woman to open her heart to a life filled with hope and joy for both her and her sister.

four

"David came to the house last night," Emily announced as she entered through Sally's back doorway. "He talked to the land agent, and it sounds as if they can work out a plan to buy a lot for the church."

"Let's sit in the kitchen," Sally urged. "You can tell me all about it while I make tea."

"The agent says they need work done on the road to Colosse. If our men will do it, then George Scriba will give us the lot behind David's store." Emily sat at the big round table.

"You mean the street that goes out to Colosse?"

Emily nodded. "Do you think instead of calling it the Colosse Road, we could rename it Church Street? I'm sure other congregations will want to build too."

Sally put the teapot on the table and reached to take cups off the shelf. "I heard there is at least one more congregation that wants a better place to meet. Do you think their men will help with the road too?"

Emily shook her head. "I don't think anyone has had time to talk to them. We are just too excited to think of having our own church building."

"Pastor came in late last night. I had gone to bed, so he didn't tell me about all this. And he left early this morning. He must be trying to let everyone know."

"How do you like having a boarder?" Emily asked.

Sally smiled and poured the tea. "Nice to have someone in the house. Been very quiet since Abbie got married and moved to Colosse."

"How is that daughter of yours?" Emily asked, sipping her tea.

"She and Daniel came to see me last Sunday after church. She looks well but is troubled by morning sickness."

"When is their child due?" Emily put down her cup.

"Not 'til fall. I've worried a bit about having the pastor here then. I'll want to go stay with Abbie when the baby is born."

"He can take his meals with us. Edie would love having him around."

"Liz tells me the girl is very taken with our new preacher. Is this a young girl's crush?"

"Oh, I suppose it could be. He is so kind to her, and she thrives on his attention."

"What about Liz?" Sally asked, looking over the rim of her teacup.

Emily scrunched her face in puzzlement. "What do you mean?"

"Every single girl in town is mooning over him. Isn't your daughter one of them?"

"No. She is kind, but, if anything, she tries to avoid him. Right now all she thinks about is teaching school. She worries about being qualified to teach. And I think she's concerned about how Meg will feel if she isn't chosen for the job."

Sally sighed and put her cup down. "The commissioners meet the first of the week. I hope Meg hasn't done something to embarrass the family."

"What can she do? They are going to look at the qualifications, and Liz has the most schooling and the best grades."

"When it comes to your sister's child, anything can happen. She's not beyond trying to discredit Liz to get the job."

"What have you heard?" Emily asked in suspicion.

"Meg is trying to spread the rumor that Liz is unstable. That she won't be able to control a classroom of children." Sally put her cup back in the saucer.

Emily sputtered midswallow, spitting out some of her tea. "Who would believe that? Liz has taught Sunday school, and the youngsters love her."

"The commissioners don't belong to our congregation," Sally reminded her.

"Then how can Meg influence them?"

"She has been asking their wives to tea."

"No," Emily exclaimed. "What can we do?"

"Oh, I know a few of the ladies, and I've made a point to speak to them."

Emily shook her head. "I'm glad my sister didn't live to see what Meg has become. The girl certainly takes after our mother." She put her cup down. "What else can we do to show Meg the Christian way?"

"We can pray she sees the light and doesn't end up like your mother."

"Meg is on her way to causing as much pain as my mother did. I hope Pastor Ames's teachings will influence the girl."

"He will be so busy building a new church, he may not have time to advise Meg." Sally got up to refill the teapot.

"Don't make more for me. I need to get back home to start supper."

"Don't you let the girls cook?" Sally asked in surprise.

"Liz is a good cook, and Edie is learning, but this afternoon Liz is working on Edie's schooling, so I told them I would cook the evening meal."

"How is Edie?" Sally asked gently.

Emily looked down at her hands. "She is so sweet. Never a word of complaint. She likes to read." Emily looked up at Sally, who still stood by the stove. "I worry what will become of her if something happens to me."

Sally sat down with a thump. "Are you ill?"

"No—old." Emily sighed. "Edie is only fifteen and will outlive me. Then what happens?"

"Liz will always be there for her sister." Sally reached across the table to take Emily's hands. "She loves that girl as much as you do."

"But Liz deserves a life of her own."

"And she will have one—she'll simply make sure it includes room for Edwina."

❧

Liz was surprised at how crowded the schoolhouse was on Sunday morning. Pastor Ames had called on many of his flock, and apparently other men had helped spread the word about the possible land acquisition. Standing before the gathering, he explained the offer of land for work.

"Mr. Scriba has offered to give us the land we require for a church building if we will repair the road to Colosse where it goes through town. We need people to volunteer to do the work," the pastor told his congregation. He turned to Liz, who stood between her father and brother. "Miss Elizabeth, will you take the names of those who are ready to sign up to help earn the land for our building?"

Feeling the blood rush to her face, Liz could only nod. When she dared to look up, she saw rage on Meg's face.

"Good," Pastor said. "Those of you who want to volunteer, meet Miss Elizabeth on your way out, and let's get this plan in action."

Turning back to the people in front of him, the pastor pointed to David Miller. "We thank you, Mr. Miller, for getting this set up for us. Now let us close with hymn number thirty-two."

As soon as the hymn ended, Liz went to the front desk to look for paper, pen, and ink. "Let me sign first." The deep voice that Liz knew so well made her look up from her search.

"You shouldn't be stealing from that desk." Meg's anger raised her voice an octave.

Liz stood silently dumbfounded as the pastor answered softly, "Miss Elizabeth is looking for the paper I put in that desk for this purpose, Miss Margaret."

Turning in a huff, Meg stalked out of the church.

"Maybe you should have asked her to do this," Liz suggested.

"I wanted you," he said, signing his name at the top of the page and handing the paper back to her with a smile. Further conversation stopped as men crowded around to sign up to work.

"You've got a lot of names there, Sis," Matthew said, looking over Liz's shoulder on the way home.

"Meg looked mean when she left the church," Edie said with concern. "Is she mad at you?"

"I certainly hope not," Liz said. "I think she just wanted to help Pastor Ames too."

"Can I help?" Edie asked.

"Of course. You can be my helper. You have to count how many people have signed up," Liz told her.

Edie groaned. "I don't do good with numbers."

"You will do just fine."

Matthew pulled his little sister's braids. "You can count just as well as Meg."

"Really?" Edie sounded pleased.

"Just do your best, Edwina," their mother said, turning around to smile at them.

"I'll do good, Mama. Liz is my teacher."

Over Sunday dinner, the Miller men talked about farmwork they needed to do and when they could spare time to work on the Colosse Road.

"Still too muddy to get any roadwork started."

"And it's too wet to plant much corn," Mama added as she set a pie on the table for dessert.

"Mama, could we have a bake sale to raise money for the church?" Liz asked.

Her mother cut the apple pie and served generous pieces as she considered the idea. "We could do that. We'll certainly need money to purchase building supplies."

"Your pie would bring a good price," Father said, taking a healthy bite of his dessert.

"You'd better talk to the pastor before we plan any sales," Mama told Liz.

Inwardly Liz groaned. How would she ever be able to avoid the pastor if her parents kept coming up with reasons for her to seek him out? "If I'm teaching school, I won't have time to organize sales," she argued, hoping this would put an end to the matter.

"If Pa and I can run the farm and give our time to fix the road, you can teach school and give your time," Matthew said through a mouthful of apple pie.

Liz cringed. "You're right. I'll leave a message for him at Aunt Sally's next time I'm in town."

Talk drifted to other subjects, but Liz remained unusually quiet. The better she got to know Pastor Ames, the more she found herself liking him. But with Meg's obvious preference for the pastor and Liz's own desire to be a teacher, such feelings would not do. If Meg suspected her cousin was the least bit interested in the pastor, she would stoop to do anything to keep Liz from having a chance with him.

Liz took a deep breath. She would have to find a way to stop these feelings. That was all there was to it. Because if her feelings continued to grow, she was confident they would only bring disaster to her in one way or another.

❧

Tuesday afternoon while the Miller men were working in the field, Mama sat in her kitchen chair knitting socks, and Liz taught Edwina her lessons in the parlor.

"Sounds like a carriage coming," Mama called to Liz. "I'll put the kettle on for tea."

I hope nothing is wrong, Liz thought as she hurried to answer the knock at the front door. People always came to the back door and through the big storage room into the kitchen. "How do you do," she greeted the gentleman at the door, recognizing him as one of the school commissioners. "Won't you come in?"

"Be pleased to do so," he answered, hat in hand. "And how are you this fine day, Miss Elizabeth Miller?" he asked.

"I'm well, thank you," she answered, standing aside and motioning him to come in.

Mama came into the parlor. "Why, hello, Mr. Howard. Welcome to our home."

He took her offered hand. "I came to talk to your daughter."

"Come into the kitchen. I have water on for tea," she invited.

Edie had scooted upstairs at the first sign of a stranger in the house. Liz looked up toward her sister, then to her mother.

"Your sister will be fine," Mama said reassuringly. "Come help me in the kitchen." She led Mr. Howard back to the kitchen, explaining as they went, "It's more comfortable in here." She motioned their guest to a seat at the big round table. "I have some apple pie. Could I interest you in a piece?"

"A piece of Emily Miller's famous apple pie! Only a fool would refuse," he said, chuckling. He held his cup out to Liz when she brought the teapot to the table. "As I mentioned before, I really came to talk to you, Miss Elizabeth." He grinned at Mama. "I volunteered to come out, hoping to enjoy your mother's cooking."

Cautiously, Liz sat at the table. She watched their guest savor his dessert.

"Every bit as good as it used to be." He looked at Liz. "Your mother used to teach the children when we had no school here. When I moved here, I was too old to attend her classes, but I never missed a chance to attend church when it met at her house." He cut off another bite of pie with his fork. "She always put out the best meals." He chuckled. "Got a lot of us to go to church, and maybe we even learned some Scripture." He rested his fork on the empty plate.

Liz looked from Mr. Howard to her mother. "Mother taught my cousins and me until the schoolhouse was built," she said.

"I did what I could until they hired someone," Mama admitted.

Liz saw a look of pain cross her mother's face and knew she was thinking of Edie. Her mother had stopped teaching to take care of her injured child.

Mr. Howard pushed back his plate and took a sip of tea. "Well, the commissioners met last night and decided we wanted another Miller as schoolmistress."

Liz put her cold hands around her cup. She held her breath, waiting for his next words.

Mr. Howard looked directly at her. "I have come to ask if you will be the schoolmistress at the Post Six School, Miss Elizabeth."

five

Liz struggled to maintain a proper sense of decorum as she accepted the job offer and joined her mother in seeing Mr. Howard off. But as soon as the commissioner left, Liz felt an overwhelming sense of joy and gave a little squeal of delight. She eagerly planned out the preparations she'd have to make.

"I can ride to school and leave my horse at Aunt Sally's," she told her mother as she set the table for supper.

"You will do no such thing," her mother said firmly. "You know what I think of women riding on horseback in town."

Liz hung her head, fighting her emotions. She knew there would be no changing her mother's mind, but she also didn't understand what was so bad about riding a horse into town. Giving a deep sigh, she spoke softly. "All right. I will take the buggy." Looking up at her mother, she added in protest, "But what about the days you need to go into town?"

Her mother's smile and twinkling eyes broke any tension left between them. "Those are the days you will walk the three miles to school."

Liz giggled and ran to hug her mother. Pressing her face against the side of her mother's, she could smell the lavender Mama always kept in her clothespress. "I guess it would not be ladylike for the teacher to arrive at school with horsehair covering her skirt."

Mama kissed Liz's cheek and said quietly, "I am very proud of you."

Liz stood back, brushing imagined lint from her skirt. "What do you think Meg will do now?"

"Nothing good," her mother said with disgust. "Your aunt

Sally and I try to talk to her, but she seems determined to cause herself grief."

Liz shook her head. "She creates so much of her own unhappiness. Why can't she see it?"

"I don't know. We'll just have to keep praying for her. We must trust the Lord to show us how to help her."

"I finished the arithmetic," Edie announced, entering the kitchen from the parlor.

"Be right there," Liz said.

"While you check my numbers, I will start peeling potatoes for supper," Edie told her sister.

"Better peel extra," their mother said. "Your father and brother have been working on the Colosse Road all day and will be very hungry tonight."

"Could I make some corn bread?" Edwina asked.

"I'm sure your father would love some," her mother agreed.

"You're getting to be a good cook," Liz said, looking up from the paper she was correcting. "And your arithmetic is well done too. You only have one mistake."

Edie turned from the pile of potato skins in front of her and smiled. "I'd rather cook than do numbers."

Mama lifted the cover from a pot of meat she had on the back of the stove. "You can do both, Edwina," she said, poking the roast venison with a long fork.

The women turned as they heard the horse and wagon pull into the yard. "Better get those potatoes cooking right away."

"Yes, Mama." Edwina poured water into the pan of potatoes to wash them before putting them on the stove.

In short order, supper was ready and the family had gathered around the table. After Father said the blessing, he and Matthew heaped food on their plates.

"Good corn bread," Matthew said. "Would you pass the apple butter?"

"Edwina made the bread," Mama said with quiet pride.

"You did good, Sister," Matthew said, spreading the apple

butter on a large chunk of bread. "Your lunch basket will bring the most money at the picnic on Saturday."

"I am not going to take a basket," the girl protested. "I thought Liz would get permission for a bake sale, not an auction. I'd be willing to bake, but I don't want to make a basket lunch."

"Why not? We need to auction as many lunches as we can to make money for the church. You can cook as well as any other girl around here," her brother declared.

Liz watched as Edie looked first at her mother and then at her father. Both parents smiled encouragement. "We can cook together," Liz offered. "That way I can take credit for your cooking," she teased her sister.

Edwina beamed at the compliments. "All right. I'll make a lunch basket. But only because it will help the church."

❧

Saturday dawned bright and sunny. Some of the men at the gathering in town grumbled about missing a good day to plant now that the ground had dried out, but most joined friends and family for a time of fellowship. The group met in the field beside Black Creek on Main Street. The stand of white birch trees offered shade, and people made use of it by spreading out their quilts to get shelter from the surprisingly warm sun.

"There's Meg," Matthew said, pointing toward their cousin. "I think she is trying to make sure Pastor knows which basket is hers."

Liz scowled. "Be nice. She's just trying to help raise money for the church."

Matthew scoffed. "Not that one. She's after the pastor."

"You make her sound manipulative."

"Well, she is," her brother insisted.

"Matthew, you know we aren't supposed to talk about others like this," Liz objected.

The two dropped the subject when they noticed their parents approaching.

"Where is Sally?" Father asked as they looked for a spot to spread their quilt.

"The pastor asked her son Tom to be auctioneer, so she's probably with Fannie and the boys. She does dote on her oldest grandson. I hope Abbie has a girl so she will have a granddaughter too."

"I'll have her oldest grandson in school," Liz said, thinking out loud.

"Hard to believe Jamie's already six, but you're right," her mother agreed. "Did you girls get your baskets up front? Looks like the auction is ready to start."

Edwina clung to Liz. "Do I have to go eat with whoever buys my basket?"

"You can ask him to come eat with the family," their mother suggested.

Tom Davis called the people to gather around. "Going to start the auction. You single men can find out who the best cooks are and help build the church at the same time."

"Who's that?" Edwina asked, pointing to a young man standing by himself.

"He works for Daniel and Abbie. Nice of him to come in from Colosse for this picnic," Mama said.

"His overalls need to be patched," Edie whispered.

Liz looked where her sister pointed. "We really shouldn't say things like that, Edie. He may not have anyone to take care of his clothes. Besides, God doesn't look at what we wear but at what we are like on the inside. We should too."

"Maybe he'll buy my basket."

One by one, the baskets were presented and bid upon. When Tom held up the fancy basket with pink ribbons and lace, a loud "oh" of appreciation went up from the crowd. The bidding started quickly but soon seemed to fizzle out.

Matthew poked Liz in the ribs. "Everyone knows it's Meg's, and no one wants to get stuck with her."

"Why don't you bid? After all the nasty things you say about her, you should try to be nice," his sister suggested.

Matthew raised the bid by twenty-five cents. He gave a sigh

of relief when Daniel's hired hand topped his offer. Once the bid reached a dollar, no one would go higher, so Daniel's hired hand claimed the basket and Meg.

"Look at her," Mama hissed. "She's being positively rude to that man, and he paid a dollar for her lunch basket."

"Well, we know Mattie filled the basket, so at least the man will get a good meal," Father said.

Mama rolled her eyes at him. "Men. All you think about is your stomach," she protested.

"Look, it's my basket," Edie interrupted, her voice full of excitement.

Bidding went fast. Pastor Ames kept going higher and higher, finally paying a dollar and a half to claim the basket. Liz hugged her sister when he went forward to claim his prize. Edie glowed. "I'm not afraid to sit down with the pastor."

"Go up and ask him to join us, Edie," her mother instructed.

Liz went with her sister, who was hesitant about walking with her limp in front of so many people.

By the time the girls had returned with the pastor, bidding had begun on the next basket, and Liz noticed Matthew was eagerly joining in. Her attention was distracted from the bidding for a moment as her parents greeted Pastor Ames.

"Sold!" Tom cried from the front, and Matthew announced to Father, "I got this basket. I'll be back later."

Liz laughed at her brother as he passed her. "How did you know that belonged to Jane Hancox?"

His blush made her laugh harder until she saw her own basket go up for auction. The bidding climbed steadily. Liz stood on tiptoe to see who kept running the bids up.

"Sold for two dollars," Tom shouted.

"Uncle David," Liz exclaimed, running to his side. "I didn't think you would bid," she told him.

"I'm single, so I can pick any basket I can pay for," he teased, putting his arm around her waist. "And I know who the best cooks are."

"Did Mother put you up to this?"

"You'll have to ask her. All I know is Phillip is off to have lunch with Susan Whitney, and Meg is enjoying lunch with Daniel's hired hand. I didn't have lunch, and I'm hungry."

"I'm glad you got my basket," Liz confided. "Now please come join the family. That way you'll get some of the cooking of all the Miller women."

"Sounds good to me."

Edie and Liz spread out the food in their baskets along with the food their mother had packed. "Enough to feed the whole crowd," David exclaimed, filling his plate.

"The auction went well," Pastor Ames said joyfully. "I'm sure we'll have enough money now to buy materials to start the church." Taking a bite of fried chicken, he looked at Edwina. "Did you cook this?" he asked.

She nodded her head. "Liz and I did it together."

"Edie did the work. I just made sure it didn't burn," Liz admitted. "She made the cake too."

"I'll be sure to save room for that," the pastor said to Liz.

His eyes, dark as midnight, sent shivers down her spine. She ducked her head and pretended to be looking for something in one of the baskets. *Dear God, I prayed he wouldn't buy my basket. Now I have to sit close to him anyway.* She saw the sparkle in her mother's eyes and wondered if Mama hadn't planned the whole thing. *Doesn't she know how hard it is for me to be around him? I don't have time for a beau. I'm a teacher.*

"Here comes Sally with Jamie," Mama said. "That boy certainly has his father's copper-colored hair. I wonder if Abbie's baby will inherit the red curls too."

The boy held tightly to his grandmother's hand as they joined the group. "We have lots of food. Will you join us?" Mama invited.

"Oh, my. No, thank you," Aunt Sally said, patting her stomach. "Fannie had lots of food for all of us."

Pastor Ames had jumped to his feet. "I appreciate your son being auctioneer."

Aunt Sally nodded to him and turned to Liz. "I wanted Jamie to meet his new teacher. How soon before school starts?"

"The boys need to help with haying, so we'll start the first of August." Liz took Jamie's hand. "I look forward to having you in class."

Jamie smiled and shyly shook her hand. "I promised Mama I would behave."

Liz patted him on the head. "I'm sure you will."

"Tom joined us to eat just before Jamie and I left to take our walk," Aunt Sally told the pastor. "He said you made fifty dollars."

"I didn't count that much. Maybe I missed a bid or two," the pastor said.

"Maybe some men put extra in the pot," Father suggested. "We all want a church building, and some of the men can't give as much time working on the road as they would like to."

"I'd like to go thank the auctioneer," Pastor Ames said. "Will you girls walk with me?" he asked, looking at Liz and Edwina.

Edwina was on her feet reaching for her sister's hand. Liz pasted on a smile and took Edie's outstretched hand. No matter how hard she tried, it seemed she couldn't avoid spending time with the pastor.

As Liz rose to start their walk, Meg stormed up to Uncle David. "I want to go home now," she demanded.

"I'm not ready to leave," he said calmly. "I haven't even had any dessert yet. Won't you sit down and have some cake with us?" David offered his daughter a piece of cake from Liz's basket.

"After Liz stole my job, you want me to sit down with her family? I'm going home." Meg flounced off without a word of greeting to any of her kin.

Uncle David sighed. "I would apologize, but you know she'll just do it again. She isn't a bit like her sweet mother," he lamented.

"What happened to the young man who bought her basket?" Mama tried to find his face in the crowd. "Oh, good. Matthew and Jane have asked him to join them." She looked at Uncle David. "Should I go ask them if they'd like some cake?"

Father smiled and patted Mama's hand. As Liz left with the pastor and Edwina to find Tom Davis, she heard Father say softly to Mama, "Leave the young ones alone. You've done enough matchmaking for the day."

Liz sighed. Wouldn't anyone realize she needed to focus her time on becoming a good teacher, not in finding a husband?

six

Liz daydreamed as she drove the buggy through the pastoral countryside to school. The August sun shone bright in the blue sky. *Going to be hot today. I'll let the children go home early so they can go for a swim in the creek.* Clicking the reins over the mare, she thought of the men working on the new church. *Be hot for them too. Oh, but I thank You, Lord, that Pastor Ames is so busy working there he doesn't come by the house as often. With my teaching and Edwina, I won't have time for a beau for at least a few years, but I'm afraid the pastor could weaken my resolve.*

She pulled the buggy into Aunt Sally's yard and unhitched the horse. Leading the mare to the barn, she heard Aunt Sally call from the back door. "Do you have time to visit?"

Liz shut the barn door and came to the foot of the back steps. "I'd better get to school. Some of the girls come in early, and I should have the door open for them. Maybe I'll have a few minutes this afternoon." She waved as she walked toward the Post Six School building.

"Good morning, Miss Miller," two of the girls greeted her.

"Hello," Jamie Davis shouted, running down the path. "Am I late?"

Liz fought the impulse to grab the boy in a hug. His bright, red blond curls and vivid blue eyes marked him as a Davis. Her mother had told her Aunt Sally's hair had been the same red gold when she'd married Liz's grandfather. "No, I'm just opening the door. You may stay out and play if you wish."

"No. I want to show you my arithmetic." Jamie waved his slate in front of her.

"I'll look at it right now," Liz said, taking the slate Jamie held out to her.

Elizabeth Miller's day had started. Her students were at various levels of learning. She worked with each of them, encouraging and correcting. Feeling a rumble of hunger in her stomach, she looked at the schoolhouse clock. "Time for lunch and recess."

The building grew hotter as the afternoon wore on. "I'm going to excuse you early today, students. You've been very good, and now you should be able to enjoy the rest of the afternoon outside."

A whoop of joy echoed through the room as the youngsters trooped out the door. Liz smiled and started to gather up her papers.

Walking the short distance to where her horse waited in Aunt Sally's barn, Liz thought about lessons for the next day. She saw a note on Aunt Sally's back door.

Took some cold tea to the workers at the church.

"I'll just head home and see if I can help Mama," Liz decided. She hitched her horse to the buggy and started down the road. With her father and brother spending more time helping with the church building, some of the farmwork fell to the women, and Liz figured she would clean up the bean bed before the weeds got out of hand.

Pulling into the barnyard, Liz looked up with a start when the back door slammed. Edie ran toward her.

"Oh, Liz! I prayed you would come home early. I need you. Mama is hurt!"

"What?" Liz twisted the reins around the buggy seat and leaped down. "Where's Mama?"

"In the house," her sister wailed. "She's sitting in her chair in the kitchen, napping, I think."

Liz put her hand against Edie's cheek. "Slow down and tell me what happened while I unhitch the horse."

Edie followed right behind Liz, explaining to her sister. "We went to weed the garden. I did the carrots, and Mama started in the bean patch. I did not hear her call, but I went to see if she needed me and found her sitting in the dirt." Tears streamed down the girl's cheeks. "She could not get up."

Liz turned the mare out to pasture. "Did she talk to you? What did she say?"

"She said her back hurt. I helped her get up, but she had to hang on to me to get back to the house." Edie continued to cry. "I didn't know what to do. I helped her into her chair and made some tea."

"You did fine, Edie. Now let me go see what else we can do." Liz ran to the house. Her mother sat just as Edie said. Fear clutched Liz's heart. Mama wasn't even knitting. Her mother never sat idly while there was work to be done. She knelt at her mother's side. "Mama, I'm home. What can I do for you?"

Mama opened her eyes and smiled. "I must have been napping. Is it time for school to be out?"

"No. It's so hot I let the children go early. Please tell me what is wrong." She took her mother's hands.

"I hurt my back." She chuckled softly. "Must be old age."

"Did you fall? How did you hurt your back?" Liz insisted.

"I twisted around to reach the bucket and something popped. All I could do was sit down and hope the pain would go away."

"Did it?" Liz demanded.

Her mother looked chagrined. "It's not too bad if I don't move." She squeezed her daughter's hands. "I will be all right tomorrow. Now we need to get supper for your father."

"I've already started," Edie said from behind her sister. "I picked the new beans and pulled some carrots. Before we went out to weed, you put salt pork in water to freshen. I could make biscuits," the girl offered.

"You have everything so well in hand, you don't need me," Mama said, a look of pride on her face.

Edie fell at her mother's feet and started to sob. "Mama, I do need you. I cannot do anything without you."

Mama looked up at Liz as she put her arms around the weeping girl. "She got me in the house and has waited on me as if I were a queen. I'm the one who needs her." She brushed Edie's hair back from her face. "We need each other, Edie. Now dry your tears and go make a big batch of your special biscuits for your father."

Smiling through her tears, Edie wiped her face with her apron. "Do you feel better, Mama?"

She nodded her head. "I will be fine, Dear."

Watching Edie scurry off to start supper, Liz again knelt next to her mother. "What are we going to do? Should I go fetch Polly Wheeler?"

"Not yet. If I'm not better tomorrow, we will ask her to come."

Liz stood and wrung her hands. "How will I let the children know there is no school tomorrow?"

"There will be school, and you will teach it." Her mother motioned toward Edwina. "I have someone to look after me."

"But she can't hitch the horse to the buggy and go for help."

"If I'm not up to weeding the rest of the beans tomorrow, I'm sure your father will insist on staying home." Her chestnut-colored eyes held a dreamy look. "He has always been there when I needed him. He will be now."

Liz had the table set, and Edie had made milk gravy with fried salt pork to go with the biscuits by the time their father and brother got home.

Liz watched her father's face when he came through the back door. He seemed to sense her mother's pain. The look of love and concern that passed between her parents twisted Liz's heart. *I hope someone will love me like that someday.*

"What happened, Emily? You look so pale." Father leaned over her, a look of concern on his face.

"I twisted my back. Should be fine tomorrow."

"What were you doing?" he asked suspiciously.

"We were weeding the garden," Edie told him quietly.

Father sighed and knelt down. "I asked you to wait 'til I could get it done. You have always tried to work as hard as any man I know. My sweet wife, you need to slow down."

"Are you telling me I am getting old?" she asked in mock anger.

He leaned over to kiss her. "Not to me," Liz heard him whisper in her mother's ear.

"Supper's ready," Edie announced.

When Mama tried to stand, her face went white. Father immediately whisked her into his arms and carried her to the table.

Matthew came in from unhitching the oxen in time to see his mother being seated at the table. Quickly Liz told him what had happened.

"Sit down, children, so we can have the blessing," Father called to them. Before he blessed the food, he asked God to heal Mama.

"What about tomorrow, Pa?" Matthew asked, piling milk gravy on a plate of biscuits.

"No reason you can't go work on the church. I'll stay here to keep track of your mother." He smiled and patted her hand. "Can't trust her alone. She might be out trying to bring in more hay."

"I could stay home from school," Liz offered.

Her father looked stern. "You have a job to do. See that your charges learn their lessons, and I will take care of the family and the farm."

"I can take care of the house and cook," Edie said confidently.

"Yes, you can, Edwina. Until Mother is better, you are in charge of the house."

Edie beamed. Watching her sister straighten her back, Liz suddenly realized the girl was growing up before her eyes.

❧

Liz got up early the next morning, but Edie already had breakfast started when she walked into the kitchen. "Coffee is ready," her sister told her, pointing to the stove.

"I'll fix my lunch," Liz said, pouring a cup of coffee. "Do you need anything from town?"

"Don't think so."

"You take the buggy as usual, Liz," her father instructed. "I will ride my mare into town."

"Do you want me to go by Wheelers'?"

"No, but you could let your aunt Sally know your mother is hurt."

Father accepted the plate of eggs Edie handed him. "You're doing fine, Edie. Could I have a cup of coffee too?"

Edie bustled to serve him. "Should I take Mama a cup of tea?"

"Good idea," he said, taking the coffee Edwina offered him.

Liz wrapped bread and cheese in a piece of cloth and swallowed the last of her coffee. "I'll get an early start. Are you sure you don't want me to stay home?"

Her father motioned to Edwina. "We are well cared for, thank you."

Matthew sat down to the plate of food Edie put in front of him. "Edie, you can cook as good as Mama," he said, shoveling bread and eggs onto his fork.

Surprised at how well the morning seemed to be starting off without her assistance, Liz headed out the door for school. Maybe it was time for her to stop thinking of Edie as so dependent on others for everything.

❧

Liz took time to tell Aunt Sally what had happened before she started to school. The day seemed to drag on for hours longer than it should. Finally she excused her students and hurried home.

She saw Aunt Sally's buggy in the yard and breathed a sigh of relief. "Maybe she can help," she told the mare as she turned the horse into the pasture.

Entering the kitchen, she stopped to watch her sister serve Polly Wheeler and Aunt Sally cookies and tea. Pride in her sister filled Liz's heart. "Hello," she called to the two older ladies. "Where's my mother?"

"Polly has her in bed with a poultice on her back," Aunt Sally replied. "She'll rest easier now."

Liz dropped into a chair with a sigh. "I hope so. Mother never gets sick."

"Your mother has worked hard all her life, and her backbone has finally told her to slow down," Polly Wheeler said.

"I can hear every word you say, so watch who you are talking about," Mama called from the bedroom off the kitchen.

Liz jumped up and ran to her mother. "Are you better? Can I get you anything?"

Mama smiled and reached to take Liz's hand. "I'm just fine. Polly wants me to lie flat for a few days with this poultice on my back."

"Will you do it?" Liz asked.

"Oh, I'll keep the poultice on, but I may move to my chair in the kitchen. Can't do anything lying here," her mother grumbled.

Liz laughed, "If you're complaining, you must be feeling better."

Mrs. Wheeler came to the door. The old lady's body bent with age, but her wrinkled face glowed with good will. Putting a hand on Liz's shoulder, she asked, "Think you can keep her down a day or two?"

"She's already talking about sitting in her chair in the kitchen."

"Stop talking as if I wasn't here," Mama scolded. She smiled at her old friend. "I appreciate your coming, Polly. The pain will make sure I take it easy, even without you giving me orders."

"You have two good girls to take care of you," Polly said.

"It's my sister who is doing the most. I'm off teaching school," Liz explained.

"Edwina can take care of your mother. You take care of your students," Polly stated.

"Would you like some tea?" Edie asked, joining the women in the bedroom. Looking at her sister, she added, "Mrs. Wheeler taught me to make the poultice for mother's back."

"I'm very proud of you, Edie," Liz said. As through a blur of tears she watched her sister serve tea to their visitors, Liz realized it was time to focus on what Edie could do rather than on her limitations.

seven

Each morning when Liz parked her buggy at Aunt Sally's, the older lady was waiting to hear about Mama. Liz made a point of coming a few minutes early so she'd have time for a quick visit.

"Mama is getting around more," she reported one morning. "Father carved her a cane." Liz felt the tears behind her eyes. "It is so sad to see her leaning on a cane. She has always preferred to run."

"That's why her back gave out. Tiny little thing climbed the ladder and helped your father build their first cabin." Aunt Sally shook her head. "She took care of Beth until she died."

"She isn't going to die is she?" Liz voiced the fear that had clutched at her heart for days.

"Not from a hurt back. If she takes care and doesn't strain it again, she'll be fine."

"Now she's worried about the crops. Things have to be preserved for winter. Edie is doing everything she can, but Mama chafes at not being able to help more."

Pastor Ames appeared behind Aunt Sally, who stood in the kitchen doorway. "How is your mother?" he asked.

"Better, thank you." Liz stared at her feet. She couldn't look at this man without her heart refusing to beat properly.

"And how is your sister?"

Startled, Liz looked up.

"Is Edie all right?" the pastor asked.

"She's taken over running the house. She cooks, takes care of Mother, and now she is putting vegetables away for winter." Pride in Edwina overcame the constant feelings of embarrassment Liz felt whenever she was near Pastor Ames.

"I'll go out to see them today," he said. "You know, Edwina is one of God's special people."

Liz nodded her head. "She certainly is special to my family. I don't know what we would do without her right now, and I'm sure both Edie and Mother would welcome a visit." She straightened her sunbonnet. "I must get to school. The children will be waiting for me."

❧

With September came cooler weather. The schoolhouse did not feel so much like an oven. But Liz noticed increasing numbers of the older children were missing. They were needed at home to harvest crops.

"Salmon are running, Miss Miller," Jamie shouted as he burst through the doorway one morning. "Can't have school today. You gonna catch salmon?"

Liz tousled his curly hair. "I guess if my family is to eat this winter, I'd better help catch salmon. You run along to help. I'll wait until I'm sure no children are coming today."

A short time later, Liz walked to Aunt Sally's. Before she hitched up her mare, Liz looked in Aunt Sally's back door. "The salmon are running," she called. "You want to come with me?"

Aunt Sally came to the door. "I can't wade in the water and catch them, but I can still put them down in salt. Does Edwina know how to cook a fresh fish?"

"Mama will be there to tell her. Come on, let's go fishing."

Families gathered at various spots up and down Salmon Creek on the eastern edge of town. "With Matthew's appetite, we'd better put down an extra barrel this year," Father announced. Mama had allowed him to carry her from the wagon to the riverbank so she could watch the proceedings.

"We came to help," Liz called from the buggy.

"No school?" her father asked.

"No children showed up. They are all fishing, so I picked up Aunt Sally, and here we are, ready to fish."

"I can't pull up my skirts and go in the water," Edie whispered to her sister.

Liz hugged her sister, understanding the girl's embarrassment over the scars on her legs. "You catch the ones we throw on the bank. Aunt Sally will show you how to knock them in the head and pile them up for the men to clean."

Tucking up her own skirts, Liz joined her father and brother in the water.

"What can I do?" an all-too-familiar voice asked.

Liz froze at the sound. The waters felt warm compared to what fear did to her heart. *Why did he have to pick my family to come to?*

"Welcome, Pastor," Father called. "Come on down here. We'll show you how to spear salmon."

Fighting back the feelings pulsing through her, Liz continued to work at her brother's side.

"You all right, Liz?" Matthew asked as he tossed another fish toward Edie. "You're so quiet."

"My feet are cold," she muttered.

"Pa and I can spear enough fish. Go help Edie stack them," her brother urged.

Liz looked down. Her feet were bare, her wet skirts were tucked up and dripping. *If I stay here, Pastor won't be able to see my legs.* "I'm all right," she told her brother, grabbing another fish.

"Don't take a chill," Matthew warned.

They continued to toss fish to Aunt Sally and Edie on the bank. Mama sat close enough to them to help pile the fish to be cleaned. "Take time out for lunch," she called.

"Mama made doughnuts this morning," Edie added.

"And I brought cheese," Aunt Sally offered.

"Sounds good to me," Pastor said, coming out of the water. "I've never fished this way before. It's fun." He took one of the doughnuts and a chunk of cheese that Edie offered him. "You make the best cheese I ever tasted," he told Aunt Sally, taking another big bite.

"That's why her daughter and son-in-law expanded the creamery at Colosse. Sally couldn't make it fast enough to keep up with the demand," Mama said, holding the pan of doughnuts out to her husband.

Liz hesitated on the riverbank. Finally swallowing hard and ordering her heart to behave, she walked to the quilt spread out and set with food.

"No school today?" Pastor Ames asked, sitting down next to her.

His voice sent shivers up her spine. "The children are helping their families. Everything stops when the salmon come up the river." Liz was relieved she managed to get her two sentences out. Her mouth was inexplicably dry, and the doughnut she was eating tasted like sand.

❧

Stephen Ames absently took the doughnut Edie offered him and turned to Liz. No matter what he did or said, he could hardly ever get her to look at him, and he wondered what he could possibly have done to offend her or scare her. Shaking his head in confusion, he took a bite of the fried cake.

The breeze ruffled Liz's blond hair. It had come loose as she worked in the stream, and as it flowed down her back, the hair reminded Stephen of ripe wheat rippling in the field. *She is so beautiful. She is compassionate and loving toward everyone but me.*

As if she heard his thoughts, Liz looked up. Her eyes were the color of strong tea.

"Would you like some water to drink?" he asked.

Quickly looking down at her uneaten lunch, Liz shook her head.

"Liz, why do you avoid me? Have I done something wrong?" he asked softly.

Her blush sent a warm glow through him. Liz spoke so quietly, he had to lean toward her to hear her words.

"You are very kind to Edwina. I thank you for that."

"But why can't you and I be friends?" he insisted.

Stephen Ames thought he saw tears in her eyes before she turned away. He watched in amazement as Liz jumped up.

"I need to help my mother."

Puzzled and saddened by the rebuff, he sighed deeply and finished eating his lunch.

"Want to learn to clean fish?" Matthew called over to him.

"I learned to clean fish when I lived on the coast of Connecticut. Want to see who can clean the most?" Stephen challenged the young man. He got up, leaving thoughts of Liz in the back of his mind.

"Save a couple big ones, and we'll cook them over an open fire for supper," Sally told the men.

Jonathan looked up from the fish he held. "Pa used to do that every year."

Sally smiled. "Your father said he learned to cook fish over a fire from an Indian friend."

Stephen helped with the work but kept watching Liz whenever he could. He wondered if she felt the attraction toward him that he definitely felt for her. Maybe she was afraid to acknowledge it because she thought no one could love her enough to accept her feelings of responsibility for Edwina as well. He'd certainly seen evidence of how much she cared for her younger sister.

Edie bent down to pick up the fish that were cleaned. "Mama says I am to wash them in the creek and pile them in the bags to go home. Then we will put them down in salt for winter."

"Do you know how to do that?" Stephen smiled at the girl's enthusiasm. She kept her wild curly hair braided tight and wound around her head.

"No, but I will learn," she told him in a determined voice.

"I'm sure you will." He smiled encouragement at her.

"You are the first stranger she has made friends with," Jonathan remarked, watching Edie carry fish to the creek.

"She's sweet. People like her sense who cares for them," Stephen observed, watching the girl put salmon fillets into bags.

"That's true," Jonathan agreed. "Well, I'd better go get Emily back to the house. The pain leaves her more tired than she will admit."

Watching Jonathan gently pick up his wife and carry her up the riverbank to the waiting buggy, Stephen took a moment to pray silently for the woman. *God, bring her peace and comfort in her affliction.*

Eager as a puppy, Edwina followed her parents and handed her mother her cane. "Aunt Sally will ride with you, Mama. I'll run home and start supper."

Stephen helped the men clean up the riverbank where they had buried the fish guts. Then he picked up a sack to carry back to the farmhouse. He stole glances at Liz as she picked up the lunch scraps and folded the quilts they had sat on.

"May I help you carry that?" he offered, seeing her bundle.

"I can manage, thank you. I'm sure Matthew would like help with the bags of fish."

Once again Liz turned away without looking into his face. Stephen sighed and went to help Matthew.

"You are coming to supper with us, aren't you?" Jonathan invited. "The best salmon is fresh caught and cooked outside. That's precisely what we're having tonight." He smiled. "And Liz made berry pies last night."

"I'd like that, Jonathan, but I'm not sure Liz would. She seems to try to avoid me," Stephen confessed.

"You never can know about these women. Liz's mother followed me into the wilderness before we got married. But Liz may think it would be too bold to show an interest. Some women show their feelings and others don't."

"Liz is afraid of hurting Cousin Meg," Matthew observed.

More confused than ever, Stephen turned to Matthew. "What are you saying? What has Meg to do with your sister avoiding me?"

"Meg always gets her own way, and Liz thinks our cousin wants you," Matthew replied.

"But I'm not courting anyone. Why would either girl think I had decided on someone to pursue?"

Matthew grinned. "I don't understand women either. I just know Liz would stand aside if she were interested in anything or anyone she thought Meg wanted. She would never show an interest in you until she was sure it would not offend her cousin."

Stephen shook his head in confusion.

"Give Liz time, Pastor," Jonathan advised. "She will do what the good Lord tells her. But it will take some time. Right now she's caught up in her lessons at the school and her concerns for her sister. Ever since Edie got burned, Liz has felt responsible for her sister, on occasion to the point where she denies herself friendships and activities she'd like because she wants to be available for Edie. Sometimes I think she believes she was at fault when Edie got burned, even though we've all reassured her she did no wrong."

"I would never take her away from Edwina," Stephen protested.

Jonathan smiled. "I don't think anyone could. My Elizabeth is a lot like her mother. Emily stood by her sister till Beth died. I don't think Beth would have survived a year in the wilderness if Emily hadn't come with her." He turned with a thoughtful look. "My daughters are almost that close. Edie would not be happy without her sister close by."

"I hope that someday Liz realizes she can be available to her sister and still pursue other interests and friendships," Stephen said wistfully.

"Her mother and I have been working to that end," Jonathan said, "but sometimes it takes longer than we'd like for God to work in someone, and I think this is one of those instances. We all need to be patient."

eight

Working quickly, the men layered the fish and salt in barrels, while the women prepared supper. Now the barrels of fish were ready to be stored in the cellar Jonathan had built in the side of a hill near the barn. "This is unique," Stephen remarked.

"Always used a root cellar, but when I built this place, I made one a little fancier," Jonathan explained. He pointed to the sloping ramp dug into the ground. "Took awhile to dig it out. I moved the dirt over to a low spot by the barn. The walls are flat rock from the chimney in the old cabin."

"Plus a whole lot more we brought from the creek," Matthew stated.

Jonathan slapped his son on the back. "You just think so because you were only a little boy when you helped haul rock."

"Come have some pie," Aunt Sally called from the house.

"Sounds good to me." Pastor put a barrel next to the one Jonathan had placed by the wall and followed the other men out of the cellar. "That fish sure tasted good. Never had salmon cooked over an open fire like that."

"Grandpa was friends with an Indian who taught him how to fasten the fish to a piece of bark and set it close to the fire," Matthew explained. "Hey, Edie," he called to his sister, who shook a cloth out the back door. "Did you have to scare off the bears to pick berries for pie?"

"No." She giggled. "I got two buckets this week, so you'll have pie next winter."

"Don't try to frighten her with your talk about bears," Emily protested as the men came into the kitchen.

"Not me," Matthew grinned. "But you know there are bears around here."

"Mama got chased by a bear years ago, and no one will let her forget it," Liz said quietly, handing Stephen a plate of pie as he sat at the table.

"So is there still a danger from bears?" he asked, taking the pie.

"They don't bother us. They like to get the apples that fall on the ground. Father leaves a few just for the animals to feed on."

"We put apples and hay out in the winter for the deer," Edwina added, joining her sister and Stephen at the table.

"The herds have kept us fed for years. It's the least I can do in return," Jonathan explained. He took a bite of pie. "As good as your ma's," he told Liz. "Where is your mother, by the way?"

"Mama is resting, and Aunt Sally took her a cup of tea. I'll get some more coffee for us." Quickly she went to the stove. Taking the coffeepot off the big iron stove, she offered to refill the men's cups, which they took outside to drink.

"Your mother is taking a nap," Aunt Sally said, coming into the kitchen from the bedroom. She started to gather plates from the table. "Your pie was very good, Liz. Did the pastor like it?"

Liz swallowed, trying to choke back her frustration. "He said it was good." She looked up from pouring the hot water into the dishpan. "He also liked the salmon you cooked."

"He's a good man. We're lucky to have him."

I can't get away from him, Liz thought, clenching her fists in frustration. *Everyone seems to push him toward me. It can't be. With Mother hurt, the school, and Edwina, my family needs me. I can't fall in love.* Turning from the table, she sighed deeply. "Edie will you see if the men want more coffee? Then we can wash the dishes." She hoped these routine chores would keep her mind off the pastor, but somehow she doubted her tactic would work.

❧

By the end of September, the town's families had their fish salted or smoked. The children were back in school. Each day as Liz hurried home from teaching, she noticed how the leaves were turning shades of rose red and gold. *The beauty of the Lord's world,* she thought, unhitching the mare and preparing to help with the harvest. Matthew dug potatoes while she and Edie picked them up and carried them to the bins in the root cellar.

"Apples are ready to pick," their father announced at supper that night.

"How will we manage?" Mama asked.

Liz looked at her mother's face and winced at the pain she saw there. "I have been instructed to close school for two weeks when the apples are ripe. Edie and I can get them ready for the dryers. Once the slices are dried, the men can pack them to ship."

"Not like the old days, Emily, when you had to pare them by hand and hang them on a line to dry," Father said, giving her an encouraging smile.

"I cooked jam from the berries, Mama. I can make apple butter if you tell me how," Edie offered with eagerness.

Liz noted how her mother's once-glowing face had lost its luster. New lines seemed to appear each day. She placed her hand over her mother's. "We will do just fine, Mama."

"I suppose Sally will come help," Mama said as if thinking out loud.

"The same boys that picked last year will be back," Matthew added. "I saw Calvin today, and he asked when you would want him and his brother."

The family looked up at Mama's deep sigh. "Are you going to let them take pay in cider again?" Her stern voice made them all sit up and take notice.

"Yes, Emmy, I am," Father answered in a firm voice.

"You know they will let it ferment. That makes you part of the evil of alcohol."

Father sighed and put his cup down. "I've told you before I can't ask the people buying my sugar what they plan to do with it. Why do I have a right to ask what they are going to do with my apple cider? It isn't up to me to condemn them. God is the final judge, not me."

"I just don't like it."

Father smiled. "You never have, but we are in business, and what happens to the apples once they are sold is out of our control."

"What's ferment mean?" Edwina asked.

"We boil our cider so it stays sweet or else we let it ferment and turn to vinegar," Liz explained quietly. "Remember the year the bull got into rotten apples and acted crazy?"

Edie nodded her head.

"Those apples had fermented. Some people like to drink the cider while it is fermenting before it turns into sour vinegar. They call it hard cider."

"They do that on purpose?" Edie exclaimed in disbelief.

It was Liz's turn to nod her head.

"Do they get sick like the bull did?" Edie asked.

"Sometimes."

"Good," Edie said, banging her spoon on her plate.

The tension between parents dissolved in laughter at Edie's simple solution.

❧

Work started at dawn the first day of the apple harvest. The pickers climbed the ladders against the trees to pick the apples. They slung cloth bags over their shoulders to put the fruit in. The men climbed up and down, filling the boxes stacked at the ends of the rows.

Mama had her chair under one of the large maple trees in the yard. She took the apples from the washtub of water and cranked the hand peeler. Next Sally cut out any spots and cored the fruit before Liz carried them to the slicer to be cut into rings. Other helpers spread the sliced apple rings in big trays to go into the drying tower. After they were dried, the apples were bleached with burning sulfur and packed into fifty-pound boxes, ready to be shipped.

Edie picked up the peelings and cores to cook into apple jelly. The poorer grade apples would be saved to make mincemeat.

For days before the picking started, the women had worked to have bread and pies baked to feed the pickers. While the apples were being hauled from the trees, huge pots of stew simmered. The brick oven held crocks of salt pork and beans. While the juice cooked, Edwina made pans of biscuits to be soaked with the new jelly and apple butter.

Liz watched her mother. In years past, she had buzzed everywhere at once to be sure the harvest went smoothly. Liz went to her mother's side. "Everything is going well," she reported. "You had us well trained before the apples even ripened." She looked up and sighed when she saw the pastor arrive.

"Nice of him to come out the first day of picking," her mother said.

"All my workers are helping here," Pastor explained a few minutes later after he'd put his horse in the pasture. "There won't be any work getting done on the church till the apples are in, so I came to help."

"Welcome, Pastor," Jonathan called. "Matthew will teach you to pick apples."

❧

The harvest continued for nearly two weeks. Applesauce was sealed in crocks. Apple butter sent its spicy smell throughout the house, masking the awful smell of the bleaching process.

"Got a bumper crop this year, Pastor," Jonathan reported on the last day. "Once we get it to Oswego and onto a lake boat to ship, we should have good sales receipts. We'll have more money to put toward the church," he added as the two men walked together to join the rest of the family for a noon break.

"We've got the frame up," Pastor Ames noted. "Should be able to get the outside planks in place before the coldest weather hits."

"Think we will worship in our own building by Christmas?" Mama asked from her chair under the tree.

"That will be our goal," Pastor declared, taking a bowl of stew Edwina offered him. "Quite a task, feeding all these people." He motioned around the group gathered in the yard for the noonday meal.

"The girls have done well cooking this year," Mama said with pride. "Edwina has made all the jelly and apple butter by herself."

"I tasted some in the kitchen a little while ago. She has done a good job. I look forward to meals here this winter," Pastor said.

"You'll be taking your meals here when Sally goes to stay with her daughter."

"So she tells me. I look forward to it," he said, holding his cup for Liz to fill with coffee.

Liz smiled and quickly turned away to fill other cups. She could feel the pastor watching her as she went from one person to another.

"What will happen when the new school is built?" Clayton asked her as she filled his cup.

"That will be for the children who have finished the grades I can teach," she told him. "Are they progressing with the building?"

"Got a late start. Should have started early like you people did with your church," he replied.

Liz walked away as talk turned to whether the schools should be consolidated. Her enjoyment of the relative solitude ended abruptly when a familiar voice broke into her thoughts.

"Your father tells me the apples are shipped on the lake boats. Can you tell me where they go?"

Liz jumped, then turned to face Pastor Ames.

"I didn't mean to startle you. Your mind must have been a million miles away."

"No. I just didn't hear you come up behind me." She put the coffeepot on a bench. "The boats go as far as Chicago and Milwaukee. I think some still go to Canada. Be better for shipping once the Erie Canal goes all the way to Buffalo." She looked at him and smiled. "A lot different than when my parents came here to build on the frontier. They had to ship freight by horse-drawn wagons."

"The teacher gives a good lesson," he said, reaching to take her hand. She quickly grabbed the coffeepot and moved away.

"I need to get the other pot and refill cups."

"I have the other pot right here," Edie called. "I'll fill cups so you can visit with the pastor."

Inwardly Liz groaned, but as she watched her sister, she confided to the pastor, "Edie is working so hard. In years past she would hide in the house and not talk to the workers. Now she is cooking and serving them. I don't think she even remembers how she limps." She watched her sister with pride.

"The Lord has given her a task and the courage to do the job well." Again Pastor reached out to touch her arm. "Do you know what He has for you to do?"

The spot where he touched her burned. Trying not to show how he affected her, Liz pointed her chin upward. "He wants me to care for my sister and now my mother and teach children." She spoke firmly, hoping he would know that meant there was not a place for him in her life.

"Don't be too sure that is all," he said.

The look in his eyes sent her emotions racing. *What could he possibly mean?*

nine

The leaves fell from the huge maple trees. Bare limbs took the place of the bright colors of fall.

"Getting cold these November mornings," Father said, accepting a cup of coffee from Edie.

"Matthew got up early and got the fires going. Wanted it warm for Mama," Edie noted.

"I'll take her some tea and see if she is ready to get up," Liz said.

The family had fallen into a routine doing the things that Mama had done for years. Now Edie was the one up and bustling about to wait on them. Liz knew her mother chafed at being slowed down and hoped that the injured back would heal in time as Polly had predicted.

"Good morning," Liz said as she entered her mother's room.

"If you will give me a hand, I can get up and walk to the table for breakfast," Mama said.

Liz put the cup on the table next to the bed and offered her hands to her mother.

"Just keep your arms firm, and I can hold on to your hands and pull myself up."

Liz saw the pain the simple act of getting out of bed caused her mother.

Gasping, Mama pulled herself to her feet. "I will be fine just as soon as I get my balance." She smiled at Liz. "It's the first step that hurts so much."

Liz helped her mother dress and walked with her to the breakfast table. Edie hurried to put a plate of toasted bread and a cup of tea in front of their mother.

"I'm blessed to have such good daughters," Mama said as she

sat in the chair Father held for her. After sipping her tea, she asked Liz, "How soon does Sally plan to go stay with Abbie?"

"I'll ask her this morning. Now I have to get to school."

"I cut you some bread and cheese for a lunch." Shyly Edie held out a small package wrapped in cloth.

Liz gave her sister a hug. "You are sweet to remember. Thank you."

Driving the buggy into town, Liz thought about Aunt Sally going to be with her daughter. *That means the pastor will be at the house every day. The more I am around him, the more I know I could care for him.* With a deep sigh, she made up her mind to trust the Lord to help her be faithful to the work she had to do for her family and the school and to resist the temptation of falling in love with Pastor Ames.

❧

Before she hitched her horse to go home that afternoon, Liz knocked at Aunt Sally's kitchen door.

"Come in, Dear. We are in the parlor," Aunt Sally called when Liz opened the door.

Walking into the cozy room where a fire burned in the grate bringing warmth to the chilly day, Liz saw Meg sitting in Aunt Sally's favorite chair. Liz gave her aunt a questioning look but did not say anything.

"Find a seat and let me pour you a cup of tea," Aunt Sally instructed with a nod.

Liz got the older lady's unspoken message not to cause trouble. She sat in a straight-backed chair and took the cup Aunt Sally offered her.

"Meg has come to ask about Abbie," Aunt Sally said.

"How nice. Mother asked me to stop by and find out how soon you would be going to stay with her," Liz explained, then sipped her tea.

"Daniel came by yesterday and said Abbie was close to her time and wanted me with her. I plan to move out there on Sunday after church."

"And the pastor will move in with us while you are gone," Meg announced.

"He plans to stay right here. That way he will keep the fires going so the house will not be damp and cold when I come home." Quietly putting her cup back down, Aunt Sally continued. "And Emily has offered to have him for his meals."

"Aunt Emily is crippled. She can't cook for him," Meg protested.

"Edwina is doing the cooking," Liz said sternly.

"How can she cook?" Meg asked with disdain.

"She is a very good cook, Meg, just as you could be if you put your mind to it," Aunt Sally said firmly.

Liz saw the look of anger as Meg turned to Aunt Sally. "You compare me with her?"

"She has more kindness in her little finger than you do in your whole body," Aunt Sally said grimly. "Your mother would be ashamed of you most of the time."

Meg's face grew red. "My mother taught me to be a lady, not a drudge. I do not have to do menial work like cook and clean."

"Your mother died when you were eight years old. You were no lady then, and you are no lady now." Aunt Sally banged her cup and saucer on the table. "Edwina suffered a terrible accident, and you speak unkindly of her. What happened to her was not her fault. However, what you have made of yourself is on your conscience."

Meg stood, her hands clenched. "I came to offer the good pastor a place to stay and meals while you are gone, and you treat me like this!" Her voice had climbed an octave.

"Sit down and behave, if that is possible," Aunt Sally instructed the irate girl.

Liz looked from one to the other, not knowing what to do or say. The tea in her cup grew cold.

"I do not have to do what you tell me." Meg tossed her head. "I will talk to Pastor Ames myself."

"Did I hear my name mentioned?" Pastor called from the back door.

Liz watched fascinated at the change in Meg's demeanor.

From a red-faced harridan, she changed to looking sweet and demure. "I came to call on Aunt Sally," Meg said to the pastor, who stood in the doorway. "I was concerned what you would do while she went to stay with her daughter."

"That is nice of you," Pastor Ames said, taking the cup of tea Aunt Sally offered him. "Emily and Jonathan Miller offered to feed me some time ago. I look forward to going there, but thank you for your concern." The pastor sat down and sipped his tea.

Meg sat back down and smoothed her skirt. "I cannot imagine anyone wanting a house that has the privy inside." She never looked up from smoothing the imagined wrinkles.

Liz saw the look of disbelief on the pastor's face. "I am glad my father had the foresight to put the privy at the back of the storeroom," she said in her family's defense. "Now mother does not have to go out in the cold," she added quietly.

"I think your father has put a lot of good things in your house," the pastor said. "I, for one, am proud to be welcome there."

Meg stood up. "Well, suit yourself, Pastor, but you know you can always come to my home. Now I must be off to see about supper for my father and brother." Her lips did not touch Aunt Sally's cheek as she bent to give her a kiss. "Thank you for the tea." With her head held high, Meg exited the house.

"I am sorry," Aunt Sally said, shaking her head. "I do not know what is to become of that girl."

"She will find her way," Pastor Ames said confidently. "We must continue to pray for her. You know what the Bible says: 'He that covereth a transgression seeketh love; but he that repeateth a matter separateth very friends.' Meg needs our love and our prayers. Trust God to guide her."

"I must be going too, Aunt Sally. I'll give Mother the message that you will be going to stay with Abbie and Daniel after church." She turned toward Pastor Ames but avoided looking into his face. "We will expect you for dinner Sunday afternoon."

Pastor jumped up. "I am pleased to have seen you, Liz. Please tell your mother I look forward to being with your family while Miss Sally is away."

"Edwina will be delighted to cook for you." Liz picked up Meg's cup and her own and carried them to the kitchen. Coming back into the parlor, she quickly gave Aunt Sally a kiss and left with a wave to Pastor Ames.

❧

Sunday morning, the Millers arrived at the schoolhouse ready for church and found confusion reigned.

"We cannot find the hymn books," Pastor explained when Father asked what was wrong. "They aren't in the box where they belong."

Liz immediately looked at the shelf where the books were kept. *I know they were there Friday afternoon. What happened?*

"You might know that Liz could not take proper care of important matters," Meg said haughtily as she swished by the group. "I would be a much better teacher and not misplace a box belonging to the church," she announced to anyone who could hear.

Liz cringed at her cousin's harsh words. Jamie tugged on her skirt.

"I like Miss Elizabeth," the child said loudly. "She isn't mean like you."

Fannie rushed to pull Jamie away. She tried to hush her child and scolded him for his rude comments. Aunt Sally's smile was grim as she patted her grandson on the head.

Stepping to the front of the room, Pastor Ames motioned for everyone's attention. "We don't need hymn books for the old songs. Let's start with " 'Jesus Lover of My Soul.' " Pastor Ames's voice rang out in a strong bass to lead his congregation in song.

Liz looked around in surprise when she saw two of her students join the church service. *I thought they went to a different church. Maybe they wanted to see what went on in their classroom on Sunday.*

She forgot the incident as she tried to concentrate on Pastor's sermon and not on the man himself.

Soon after the Millers arrived home from church, Pastor

Ames arrived for dinner. Still wondering who had been in her classroom, Liz remained silent. She watched and helped Edie serve up pot roast and potatoes. Proudly, Edie served apple crisp for dessert. "Mama told me how to make the crust," she explained when everyone told her how good it tasted.

Once the meal was finished, Liz and Edie cleaned up the dishes while the men enjoyed coffee at the table. After catching up on details about the church construction project, Jonathan asked, "So what do you think happened to the hymn books?"

"I am sure it is no fault of Liz's," Stephen answered, giving her a reassuring look as she took his plate.

"I just hope my niece is not mixed up in this," Jonathan observed. "Meg seems to find ways to cause mischief, and she certainly was quick to lay blame this morning."

"She needs our prayers and direction," Stephen said. "I don't understand why she or anyone would move the hymnals. What could they hope to accomplish?"

"It's best to forget the incident," Emily said. "Whoever the guilty party is, they didn't create a significant problem, and hopefully they won't cause more mischief."

Stephen nodded, but his mind was not on hymnals. He watched Liz washing the dishes. Remembering Meg's comments that morning, he determined to find a way to protect Liz's reputation from any damage caused by her cousin.

❧

On Monday after school, Liz stopped at the mercantile to buy some thread for her mother. As she came through the door, Phillip motioned for her to move to the back of the store. Puzzled, Liz walked behind a display and waited to see what he wanted. It was then that she noticed the two boys she had seen in church.

She watched the children looking at the candy display and trying to decide what to buy.

"We got a dime apiece to spend," the towheaded lad told Phillip. "I want to give some candy to Miss Miller. She is the best teacher in the whole world."

"I'm going to eat all mine," the other boy said. "When she gave us the money, Miss Margaret said she could teach me arithmetic better than Miss Miller."

"Awe, you're too dumb to learn from anybody," his companion said.

"I found that box and moved it for Pastor Ames like Miss Margaret said to."

Liz peeked around the counter where she was hidden in time to see the first boy look puzzled. "I still don't know why she told us to do that. When we went to church on Sunday, the pastor didn't know where the books were."

"I like that pastor. I think I'll go back to the church in our schoolhouse."

The boys made their purchases and left with mouths full of candy.

Liz forgot the thread she was planning to buy and moved to the counter where Phillip stood. "What do you think of Meg now?" he asked.

Liz shook her head. "Why didn't you scold those boys?"

"They didn't know what they did was wrong. They did what Meg told them, and she paid them to do it."

"Please don't tell anyone else about this," Liz said. "If word of this spread through the community, think what it would do to Meg."

"I may not gossip with customers," Phillip agreed, "but I am going to tell my father what Meg has been up to. She shouldn't get away with it, and it's Father's place to hold her accountable."

ten

After Sally went to Colosse to await the birth of her grandchild, Pastor Ames spent nearly every evening at the Millers' table for supper.

Liz rode an emotional whirlwind. Being close to Pastor Ames and listening to him brought a warm glow to her inner being. Then she would look at her sister, who basked in the attention she gained from preparing the family meals, and feel guilty that she wasn't giving Edie her lessons, even though some of that was because Edie was too busy taking care of the house.

As she realized how proficient Edie was in covering Mama's responsibilities, Liz wondered, *Does she really need me close to her?* Quickly Liz pushed the thought from her mind. She couldn't imagine life without needing to care for Edwina.

"You're very quiet tonight, Liz," Pastor Ames commented. "Are you thinking about your students?"

She smiled weakly. "I try to be a good teacher."

"Oh, you are. I hear parents compliment you all the time."

Liz looked down at her plate and murmured, "Thank you." She could not bring herself to look at him. After Meg's maneuvering over the hymnals, Liz didn't want to think what her cousin would do if she suspected that Liz was interested in the pastor. And although she didn't like to admit it, Liz sensed that if she gave Pastor Ames any encouragement at all, he would ask her father for permission to court her.

"So how is the work going on the new building?" Father asked. "I haven't been able to help for several days."

Liz breathed a sigh of relief as talk turned to the new building.

"We have the frame up and started putting planking on the outside today. Now that harvest is over, more men are helping with the building." Pastor looked at Mama with a smile. "We still hope to be in our new church by Christmas."

"I'll be there to help tomorrow," Matthew announced.

But the next day's dawn brought dark clouds warning of a storm. Liz left her horse and buggy at Aunt Sally's but hurried to the schoolhouse before Pastor Ames could have a chance to speak to her. All her students showed up, so she kept busy all morning, checking school lessons and assigning more work.

At lunchtime she noticed the wind had come up. Some of the boys played outside, but the girls stayed inside to get out of the storm.

"Getting nasty out there, Miss Miller," Jamie announced when she called the children back for afternoon classes.

Wind whistled around the building, and rain pelted the roof. Papers rustled, and children wiggled. Liz felt their concern as the storm raged outside.

"Put your books away, and I'll read some more of *Pilgrim's Progress,"* she instructed her students.

She had just opened the book to read when the door, driven by the wind, crashed against the wall. Tom Davis grabbed it as he entered and then used all his strength to push it shut again.

"I got my wagon outside. The winds are too strong for the children to walk home safely, so I've come to fetch them home."

Voices clamored with questions. "Quiet down, children, while we listen to Mr. Davis." Liz's voice commanded attention.

Tom stood in front of the class, hat in hand. "I'll put you in my wagon and pull a canvas over you. Be some protection from the rain. Then we'll make the circuit to get you all to your homes."

"You going too, Miss Miller?" Sadie Wheeler asked.

Liz looked at Tom for his approval as she spoke. "I have my buggy at Mr. Davis's mother's house. I'll be fine." She turned her attention to her charges and told them, "Now you get your things together and do what Mr. Davis tells you. With a storm this bad, don't try to come to school tomorrow."

Quickly she helped the children gather their coats, but as she went to the door, Tom stopped her.

"You'd blow away in a minute out there. Let me take the children one by one and get them in the wagon. Then we'll worry about you."

As he spoke, the door burst open again. Pastor Ames stumbled in. "Glad to see you, Tom. Knew there would be anxious parents and came to help."

"We have the youngsters ready to go. I'm going to take them home," Tom explained. "You can help me guide them out and secure them under the canvas in my wagon."

Pastor Ames and Tom Davis soon had the children safely tucked in. "You go ahead, Tom," the pastor said. "I'll see that Miss Elizabeth gets home."

Liz stood at the window waving, but the children were under the canvas that the men had tied down over them.

God, keep them safe, she prayed.

The wind rushing in the open door startled her. Quickly Pastor pushed it closed. "I told Tom I would take you home."

"I have my buggy at Aunt Sally's. I'll be fine."

The pastor smiled. "I don't think so. The wind would blow your buggy over, and you can't walk there. You'd be blown to Colosse before you got partway."

Fear knotted Liz's stomach. "Is it that bad?"

Pastor Ames nodded. "I have my horse by the side of the building. We can ride together and get to your place."

"Edie will be terrified," Liz murmured.

"Matthew left over an hour ago to get home. He'll be there with your father to keep your mother and sister safe." He looked at the leaves whirling in the schoolyard. "We need to get going."

Liz pulled her cloak around her and held on to Pastor Ames's arm as they made their way to his horse. She only remembered winds like this one other time. It had blown the roof off Uncle David's barn. She tightened her grip on the pastor.

"I will mount and pull you up behind me," he told her.

She nodded her head and did as he said. Once on the horse, she put her arms around his waist and held on. The pastor coaxed the horse around the building into the full force of the wind.

Urging the frightened animal forward, Pastor Ames followed the road to the Miller farm. Liz clung to him as the wind tore at her cloak. The warmth of his back brought her comfort. *I could trust this man to take care of me always,* she thought. But just as quickly she remembered that other responsibilities had first claim on her.

Fear of the storm blotted out the emotion her close proximity to the pastor produced. Liz held on and prayed.

It seemed hours before they finally stopped in front of her father's barn. Matthew ran from the house to open the barn door for them.

"Ma will be glad to see you," he said, swinging the door open. "She's been fretting about both of you ever since the storm broke." He helped Liz off the horse.

"Did she think I would miss supper because of a little wind?" Pastor joked.

Liz didn't dare run to the house alone so instead stood in the shelter of her brother's arm.

"You get Liz inside. I'll take care of my horse and be right there," Pastor instructed.

Clinging to her brother, Liz made her way into the house.

Edie hugged her sister and buried her face in Liz's shoulder. "I thought you would blow away," she cried.

Liz patted the girl's back. "I was scared, Edie, but God took care of us."

"Did you see much damage?" Mama asked.

Liz laughed. "All I saw was Pastor Ames's back. Don't think I have ever prayed so hard in my life. Now I could use a cup of tea. If I don't sit down, my legs will give out right here."

Edie hurried to make a pot of tea. "I made pies this morning. Would you like a piece?" the girl offered.

Liz sank into a kitchen chair. "You sound more like Mama

every day. Can't come into this kitchen without the offer of food. I'll have some of your pie later."

"I'll try a piece," Matthew said, joining Liz at the table. "I think the pastor will too."

The wind continued to howl as the day drew to a close. "Sounds like quite a cloudburst," Father said, hearing the rain pound the side of the house.

"Are the animals all right?" Mama asked, lighting another candle on the table.

"They are restless but dry and fed. I put the milk in the milk house. It can be skimmed in the morning. I don't want you women out there tonight."

The Millers and Pastor Ames sat down for supper, and the pastor agreed to stay the night. No one wanted him to risk traveling through the storm after dark. Eventually the family drifted off to sleep through the sounds of wind whistling around the corners of the house and down the chimneys and stovepipes.

The next morning dawned sunny and bright with scarcely a breeze to speak of.

"We'll get the wagon loaded with boards and nails and start checking the neighbors," Father told Matthew and the pastor over breakfast.

"Think there will be a lot of damage?" Pastor Ames asked.

Father nodded as he put his cup down. "Had a storm like this a few years back. Lot of roofs blew off. David lost his barn roof. We'll get the men organized and start work parties to get to the worst damage first."

"I can fix bread and cheese for lunches," Edie offered.

"Good girl." Father hugged her around the waist as she circled the table to pour more coffee.

"I told the children not to go to school today," Liz said as she helped her mother to the table.

"We need to get a big pot of soup going and bake extra bread," Mama directed. "We'll need to feed the workers."

"Sounds like everyone knows what to do," the pastor said. "I want to go check on the church building."

Matthew hitched the oxen to the wagon, and then the men loaded supplies for repairs.

"I'll be home all day today, Father. You know Mother will be cared for," Liz said at the back door.

"She's doing better all the time. Can pretty much take care of herself. Just the sciatica like Polly said." He reached to take the basket of lunch Liz held out. "I should have listened to your ma a day or two ago when she said the pain was worse and a storm was coming." He patted Liz and gave her a quick kiss on the cheek. "Glad you're here. Edie was scared when that storm came up yesterday. Your presence will reassure her."

He joined Matthew and the pastor, who waited in the wagon.

Liz stood back as the men pulled out of the barnyard. Silently she prayed for those people who had suffered damage to their property. *And please, God, comfort anyone who has been hurt.*

❧

Stephen noticed how Jonathan made a point to stop at each farm on the way into town. Silas Evans and his sons were already repairing their barn.

"Cut wood shingles last winter," Silas called from the roof. "Since the wind got rid of the old ones, the boys and I will put on a new roof."

"You need help?" Jonathan asked.

"No, thanks. There will be others who need help more than we do. We'll join the repair parties as soon as we get our roof put back."

Continuing toward town, Jonathan stopped the wagon several times while Matthew and Stephen cleared tree limbs out of the road. As they approached town, they saw more people milling about. David stood in front of his store, urging people to come in for supplies.

"Did your barn hold up?" Jonathan asked his brother as he got down from his wagon.

David clapped Jonathan on his shoulder. "You did a good job.

That barn came through fine, but we did lose some shingles off the house."

"We'll get it fixed up for you," Matthew said, jumping down next to his father.

"You been to the church yet?" David asked Stephen as he joined the group gathered in front of the mercantile.

"No. I stayed at Jonathan's last night, and we just got to town."

David shook his head. "Not good, Pastor. Place looks like a pile of sticks."

"We better get over there," Jonathan said, hopping back on the wagon seat. As soon as Matthew and Stephen joined him, he drove to the church building site.

As they pulled up to the familiar spot, Stephen Ames looked on what was left of his church with shock and grief. His dream lay in shattered pieces.

He didn't remember climbing down out of the wagon, but suddenly he was standing in front of the wreckage, surrounded by several men who had been looking at what was left of the church.

"Real shame, Pastor."

"We'll get it built back up right quick," another said.

Stephen felt Jonathan's arm around his shoulder. "The Lord must have a better idea," his friend said quietly.

The school commissioner approached them. "I have a suggestion for you, Pastor."

Although Stephen had met John Howard, the man wasn't part of his congregation. Stephen tried to push back the overwhelming sorrow he felt at the damage to the church and concentrated on listening to the commissioner.

"You know we are building a brick school. We didn't get started early enough this year, but we will work through the winter. Did you know the academy building will have a first floor for community use? That includes churches."

Stephen couldn't think clearly. "I guess I heard something about it." He motioned toward the pile of lumber that had been the frame of his new church. "I didn't think I would need to use your school."

"Get your men to come work on the academy. They'll earn a little money, and the community will have a school. And you'll have a larger place to hold church services while you figure out what you want to do here."

Stephen Ames looked at what was to have been his first church building. He swallowed hard, squared his shoulders, and took Mr. Howard's offered hand. "And next summer we will complete a building of our own," he said with conviction.

The men around him cheered. Silently Stephen thanked God for giving him the courage to go on.

eleven

"Hi, Phillip," Liz greeted her cousin as she stepped into the mercantile later that week. "Mama sent me to check on Aunt Sally's house, so I stopped by to see you."

"Been lots of excitement around here."

"Father and Matthew have been doing repairs all week."

"I'll be glad when they get to our house. I'm tired of listening to my sister complain," Phillip sighed.

Surprised, Liz responded, "I didn't know your house was damaged."

"We lost a few shingles. To hear Meg, you would think the whole roof landed in the creek."

"Neither my father nor Matthew said anything about it."

"It's not serious. Pa and I put canvas over the spot in case it rains. Pa is working with the repair crews and said there are others who need work done more than we do."

"Aunt Sally's place looks fine. I had left my horse and buggy in the barn the day of the storm, but Matthew brought them home the next day."

"Did you hear from Daniel?"

Liz shook her head. "Is Cousin Abbie all right?"

Phillip laughed. "Daniel said she delivered a beautiful baby girl right in the middle of the storm. Good thing Aunt Sally was there. No doctor could have gotten to them in that deluge."

"Mama will be relieved to hear the news. She's been worried about Aunt Sally and Cousin Abbie."

"Daniel came in first thing this morning. He'll probably ride out to tell your mother about his new daughter."

Liz sighed. "I'll be glad when Aunt Sally gets back." As soon as she saw Phillip's puzzled look, she regretted her words.

Raising his eyebrows, Phillip asked, "You don't like having the pastor take his meals at your house?"

Liz felt her face flush. "He's a very nice man," she murmured. "I just miss visiting with Aunt Sally," she added lamely.

"School going to start up on Monday?"

Grateful for the change in subject, Liz brightened. "Father said they replaced the broken window yesterday. I'll stop on my way home to see how much damage the wind did inside." She smiled. "I suppose papers will be blown all over the place."

"Tell Aunt Emily hello for me. You might mention how much the men working have appreciated her sending in soup and bread for their lunches."

"I just delivered a pot of hot soup on my way into town. Edie is the one doing the cooking. She seems so happy to be helping others. This way she can send food and not have to serve it in person. She's still shy around people."

"The Lord has shown her how to serve where she is comfortable." Phillip reached for a small bag. "Take her some peppermints from me and tell her how much the town's people appreciate her." When Liz frowned, he added, "I always keep a bag of candy separate from the store's so I can give them to children or to adults who've done something special.

"She'll love this." Liz put the candy in her pocket. "Thanks so much for noticing what she's done. I'm so proud of her."

"You have reason to be," Phillip said.

❧

Liz spent the rest of the afternoon straightening up her classroom. The men who had replaced the window had picked up the broken glass as well so she sorted papers and picked up broken slates. Fortunately the books had been stored far enough away from the window so that they had not gotten wet when the rain blew in.

Looking up, Liz realized the sun had started going down. "I better get home," she muttered, taking one last look around the room. "Mother will be worried."

Her horse stood patiently by the side of the school. Patting the mare before getting in the buggy, Liz promised her an extra ration of grain. "Been a rough week for you," she said, clicking the reins to start the horse toward home.

It was nearly dark by the time she unhitched the mare and put her in a stall with the promised grain.

Edie rushed to Liz's side when she came in the kitchen from the storeroom. "You didn't come home, and I got scared."

Liz wrapped her arm around her sister's waist and kissed her cheek. "I'm sorry I worried you. Took longer than I thought it would to clean up the school." Pulling the parcel out of her pocket, she handed it to Edie. "Cousin Phillip sent this to you. He said to tell you how much the townspeople appreciate your soup and bread."

Edie opened the package of candy. "Mama, look what Cousin Phillip sent me."

Her sister's childish joy brought a glow of pleasure to Liz.

Mother sat in her chair with her knitting needles clicking in rhythm to the rocker. "Daniel came by," she told Liz.

"Phillip thought he might. Did he tell you the new baby's name?"

"They named her Abbie Rose. Daniel said the child is their autumn Rose."

Liz sighed. "Sounds romantic." Turning to her sister, who stood at the stove, she asked, "What can I do to help?"

"I made biscuits and milk gravy with salmon. There's still pie left from when you baked yesterday," Edie said.

"Your biscuits smell good, Edie. I forgot to eat lunch." Liz took plates from the shelf. "I'll set the table for you."

The men came in before Liz had finished. "Smells good, Edie," Pastor Ames told her, hanging his coat on a peg. "The soup you sent for lunch tasted wonderful. Everyone liked it."

"I brought your empty pot home," Matthew said, setting the soup pot on the shelf.

Liz stole a glance at their mother. She sat with a glow of pride, watching her youngest daughter take up supper. Looking up, she caught Liz's attention and whispered, "And we feared she would be crippled."

"A small limp is nothing," Liz said quietly as she helped her mother get up to move to the table. "She's beautiful. I just wish she were more comfortable around people."

"She was really concerned about you," Mama said, leaning on Liz's arm and walking toward the table.

"I'll always be here to take care of her," Liz said quietly.

"I pray she will not always depend on you," her mother answered as she took her seat.

After the blessing, everyone eagerly helped themselves to Edie's delicious meal.

"I think we are about finished," Pastor declared, taking biscuits off the proffered plate.

"Did you repair Uncle David's roof?" Liz asked.

Her father smiled. "Yes, Miss Margaret can quit her whining."

"Jonathan!" Mama scolded.

"Emily, the girl's maid had no roof on her house, and all Meg could see was a few shingles off her own roof."

"Perhaps she didn't realize the damage to Mattie's roof was so severe," Pastor said. "I'm sure she would have been concerned for her maid."

"Is Mattie all right?" Worry filled Mama's voice.

Father nodded his head. "We got her all fixed up. She needed a new roof anyway. This way the town could do it for her, and she didn't think it was charity."

"There has been good come out of this storm," the pastor commented.

"I feel bad about the church, Pastor," Liz's mother said, toying with her food.

He looked up and smiled. "Might be a blessing there. Mr. Howard said he couldn't get enough workers for the school, so they are way behind. Now with the church men helping, the school will be built."

"Late in the year to be laying brick," Father warned between bites.

"I signed up to work part-time," Matthew told his parents.

"You did?" Liz asked in surprise.

"Not so much to do around here in the winter. I can put in a few hours on the school and donate my wages to the church."

"That's a nice thought," Pastor said. "But maybe you'd better save some of your wages for yourself."

"Have you asked Jane?" Liz teased.

Matthew sputtered as his face turned red. "Maybe Jane wants a church to be married in," he growled.

Father laughed. "I won't get any work out of you next summer if that's the case. You'll be busy full-time building the church."

"I'm sure many men will help," the pastor said. "I don't expect them to donate their wages to the church. The extra money will help some of the families have a better Christmas," he added.

Mama looked up from her food with a sparkle in her eye. "What will we do for Christmas?"

"I can cook the dinner," Edie offered excitedly.

"I am sure you can, Dear. And we will bake lots of cookies to take to people."

"I can take you in the buggy, Mother," Liz offered.

The women started talking about recipes and who should receive Christmas goodies.

"I'd like to give my students something," Liz said.

"Could you teach your students to sing a Christmas carol for church?" Pastor asked.

Liz looked at him, and her heart skipped a beat at the smile he gave her. "Maybe we could do a Christmas pageant and invite the parents to come to the school. Not all my students belong to our congregation. That way all of the children could take part."

"That's a wonderful idea," he said, joining in the excitement of planning.

"Liz," Edie said shyly, "could we make little cloth bags and put an apple and some cookies in each one for your students?"

Liz jumped up and put her arms around her sister's shoulders as she leaned down to kiss her cheek. "Edie, that's perfect. Will you help me sew?"

Edie blushed. "I don't make the stitches straight enough."

"I'll help you keep them straight," Mama offered.

"I'll go by the mercantile tomorrow and look for cloth," Liz said.

"Meg." Mama uttered the one word and then sighed. "How could we involve Meg?"

"Invite her to dinner with her brother and Uncle David," Liz said, starting to clear plates off the table.

"She is going to want to have us to her house," Emily said.

"She can't cook," Edie protested.

"No she can't," her mother said, "but I don't see why Mattie should have to give up her Christmas to cook for us. We'll just have to find a way to have David and his children come here as they always have. We can ask Meg to bring something so she won't feel left out."

"I'll talk to David," Father said, getting up from the table.

❧

The next afternoon on her way home from school, Liz stopped at the mercantile to look for cloth. "Hello, Phillip. I hear you got your roof fixed."

"But Meg is still whining."

Liz stopped fingering the bolts of cloth and turned to Phillip. "Don't you have anything nice to say about your sister?" she protested.

"Yes, but I'm just tired of hearing her complain when so many other people are suffering from real hardships. Now she wants a new dress for Christmas."

"So what's the problem?"

"Father told her no."

Liz dropped the bolt of cloth she had been holding. Uncle David never said no to his daughter. Why would he do so now?

"He told her the money she would spend on a dress should go to the church."

"Well, having to start the building over is going to make it cost more. My brother's going to work on the new school to earn some money to donate. I'm sure Meg will understand and want to do her part too."

"I asked Father if he would give me a couple days a week off so I could work at the school too."

"If this keeps up, we'll have a bigger and better church than we dreamed of." Liz clapped her gloved hands in joy.

"Pastor should be pleased," Phillip said.

"Oh, he is."

"Matthew has been looking at a gold locket," Phillip confided, "so I don't think all his wages will go to the church. He said the pastor had told him he didn't have to give everything he earned."

"I promise not to tell," Liz said. "Hard to think of my little brother interested in a girl." She sighed. "Father will miss him around the farm if he gets married and moves away."

"What about you? Aren't you thinking of moving on?"

Leave home? How could I desert Mama and Edie? She shook her head to clear her mind before answering softly, "I'm not ready to move away from my family."

Fighting the emotions his suggestion stirred, Liz concentrated on picking out cloth to make presents for her students. "Edie is going to help me make little bags to fill with treats for my students."

"She sews too?"

Liz smiled. "Not well, but it pleases her to think she can help me."

"I know how close you are to your sister. You will just have to find a husband who will take on a new sister with his wife."

Phillip's words brought visions of Pastor Ames and Edie and of how good he was with her. Sighing deeply, she pulled a bolt of bright red cloth from the display and handed it to Phillip. *Unfulfilled dreams can bring pain,* she thought as she watched her cousin cut the material. *But sometimes dreams come true.*

twelve

A few days later, Stephen Ames stood alone, looking at what would have been the new church. Men from his congregation were gathering to clean up the storm damage.

"Why, Lord?" he murmured, looking at the partially sided wall that had blown over and taken the frame for the building with it. His heart hurt with sorrow at what might have been. *Did I want this too much? Did I push my congregation too far?*

He felt someone's hand clasp his shoulder and turned to look into Jonathan Miller's eyes. Reading the sympathy and understanding there, Stephen smiled. "What do we do now?"

Jonathan patted Stephen's shoulder before pointing to the fallen structure. "We salvage all we can to use when we start over again in the spring."

Stephen sighed. "You're right. There is no other way."

The two men turned as others rode into the clearing. "Looks like we can save a lot of the lumber," Tom Davis said, dismounting and tying his horse to a nearby bush.

Stephen concealed his sorrow as best he could and warmly greeted the men who had come to work. He followed their directions as they stacked the good pieces of lumber. The planks were put into another pile. The camaraderie of the group helped dispel his discouragement.

"I've collected canvas to put over the wood we can save," Matthew said, pulling the wagon to a stop beside the first pile of lumber. When the young man jumped down from the wagon seat, he announced, "Liz and Edie sent sandwiches for lunch."

As the men gathered around the back of the wagon to enjoy the food, Stephen Ames stood to one side and watched. *Liz. Everything I do comes back to her. I enjoy her family and want to be her friend. No, I want to be more than her friend. I have watched her with her family, with the schoolchildren, and in church. She is the kind of woman I would like as my wife. But she barely speaks to me.*

Stifling his frustration, Stephen took the sandwich Matthew handed him. Thanking the young man, he tried to join in the conversation of the men around him. Listening to the plans for building the church again, Stephen silently prayed, *Dear Lord, help me. I want to stay here and serve Your people. Is this accident a sign You want me to leave? Or am I looking for a reason to leave because I cannot stand the torment of being so close to Liz when she gives me no encouragement to be her friend?*

"I need to talk to you," David Miller said quietly.

Stephen instantly forgot his own troubles to listen to what his friend had to say.

"It's about Meg." David looked down at the uneaten sandwich in his hand. "I know I'm to blame for spoiling her. When Beth died, part of me went with her. I haven't done a good job of raising our daughter, and now I'm paying for the results."

Stephen saw tears in David's eyes and squeezed the man's arm in understanding. "What can I do to help?"

David sighed. "I don't know. You've been very patient with Meg when I know her actions toward you have not always been ladylike."

"She's never been improper," Stephen protested.

David smiled. "No, just devious. You see, I do know my daughter."

"What has brought you to me?"

"My brother talked to me and made me see I had to do something about Meg. Her actions toward Liz are out of hand."

Stephen didn't answer.

"Aunt Sally and Emily have tried to do what they could, but the girl refuses to listen to them."

"And you think she would listen to me?" Stephen asked with misgivings.

"Pastor, what I am trying to say is that if you have no interest in my daughter, please make that clear to her."

Stephen shook his head. "I don't understand."

David sighed. "My brother is sure Liz cares for you but is standing back to give Meg every chance to gain your attention. If you make it clear to my daughter that your only interest in her is as a member of your congregation, she will turn to someone else. Frankly, I think she only set her cap for you to prove she could capture your attention."

"All this is beyond me," Stephen stuttered. "I wasn't aware that your daughter expected more of me than to be a spiritual guide."

"Would you tell Meg that?"

"Why? Why do you think it is necessary?"

"Because until you do, Liz will never allow you to get close to her." David spoke so softly the pastor had to strain to hear.

Is this why Liz avoids me? Hope rose in Stephen's heart. "I don't know how I will do this, but I will try to encourage Meg to see me as a pastor and nothing else."

"Be careful. My daughter is very jealous of Liz."

Before Stephen could respond, David turned away.

With a deep sigh, Stephen Ames rejoined the men. He wasn't convince that the only reason Liz avoided him was because of her concerns about her cousin. But of one thing he was certain: Piling lumber was easy compared to understanding the young women of his congregation.

By late afternoon, the last canvas tarp had been secured over the salvaged lumber. "Got a good start on material for the new church," Jonathan declared. "Come along, Pastor. Don't want to be late for supper."

❧

The next afternoon, the pastor rode out to the Millers' farm.

Edie greeted him with delight. "I'll make some coffee."

"I came to visit your mother, Edie. I think she would rather have tea. Would you make us some?" He followed the girl into the kitchen.

"What a nice surprise," Emily said from her rocking chair.

"Don't get up," Stephen hurried to say, noting the lines of pain etched in this sweet woman's face. He pulled a kitchen chair from the table close to Emily's rocker. "I miss Sally."

Emily smiled. "Is our hospitality that bad?"

"Oh, no. I love this family, but I miss Sally's advice."

"She is a wise woman. Without her, my sister and I would never have survived the frontier."

"May I ask your advice?"

"How can I help?" Emily's sincere compassion touched the core of Stephen's being.

"Well, I don't need to know how to survive the wilderness. I just come here and Edie feeds me like a king." The pastor took the cup of tea the girl offered and took a cookie from the plate she held out to him.

"Thank you, Edwina," Mama said. "Now Pastor and I have things to talk about."

"I will go out to the milk house and churn the butter."

Stephen watched her scurry away. "She is a delight."

"Yes." Emily nodded her head. "The Lord brings good even from the tragedy of a wounded child."

Putting his cup down, Stephen Ames looked into Emily's kind face. "I have woman trouble."

Emily chuckled. "Every single girl in town has set her cap for you. You should be flattered."

"I'm not. I'm confused. I didn't come here to find a wife. I came to serve as a pastor to God's people."

Emily patted his hand. "We're a small town, and a new eligible bachelor has been a temptation to some."

"Not every girl. The one I could love avoids me."

"Jonathan told me you had spoken to him about Liz avoiding you." Emily sighed. "Ever since the accident, Liz has felt responsible for her sister. Nothing we say diminishes this. Now that I am not able to take care of the family as I once did, she is even more determined to remain at home."

"I would never ask her to abandon Edie. I could take care of both of them if the need arose. Liz as my partner and Edie as our sister." He spoke with passion.

Emily toyed with the cookie on her saucer. "I would like to see my daughters happy." She looked at the pastor kindly. "And I would welcome you into our family, but this decision has to be Elizabeth's."

"How do I get Liz to even talk to me?" he asked in exasperation. "She avoids me."

Emily laughed. The sound made Stephen smile.

"You do not say it aloud," he said, "but I see the problem is more than her feelings for Edie. Liz will do nothing that might hurt Meg."

Emily let him put her cup on the table and folded her hands in her lap. "Let me tell you a story. My sister lost a child after Phillip was born. She feared she would never have another baby. After Meg was born, my sister never regained her strength. She and David basked in the joy of their little girl. The child lacked for nothing. You see," Emily's face had a dreamy look, "David loved his wife and wanted her happy. If spoiling Meg brought Beth pleasure, David saw to it that his daughter got anything she wanted."

"Not good for the child," Stephen muttered.

Emily nodded her head. "After Beth died, I think David would look at Meg and see Beth. He tended to avoid the child, and Meg resorted to misbehaving to gain his attention. She has grown up doing devious things just to be noticed."

" 'Forwardness is in his heart, he deviseth mischief continually; he soweth discord,' " Stephen quoted from Proverbs.

Emily nodded her head. "That's Meg."

"David wants me to talk to his daughter, but I don't know what to say or do."

"Don't feel badly. Neither Sally nor I have known how to treat the girl over the years. When we suggested discipline to him, David objected. I'm encouraged that he has spoken to you. At least he's recognized there is a problem."

Stephen felt stricken. "I have no idea what to do."

Emily reached over to pat his hand. "We will start by praying about it." She sat back in her rocker.

"The rewards of grateful people would be the kind of attention Meg should seek," Stephen said quietly. "I will suggest her father encourage his daughter to try helping people."

"I won't mention our talk to Liz, but I will suggest she try to interest her cousin in some acts of service. It won't happen quickly, but we will pray and work on changing Meg's attitude." Emily chuckled. "Sometimes I think it would be easier to move mountains."

"But our faith can do that too," Stephen said.

❧

That evening after supper, the men went into the parlor to talk about the work they had done that day.

"I would like a word with you," Mama said as Liz helped her mother back to her chair. "Have Edie work on hemming the Christmas bags so we can have a moment together."

"Yes, Mama." Liz got the sewing out and helped her sister get started on the bright red cloth.

Sitting on a footstool in front of her mother, Liz asked, "What is it? Do you need me to do something?"

Her mother nodded. "I have an impossible task for you."

Liz joined in her mother's infectious laughter. "What do you have in mind?"

"I am going to ask you to talk to Meg."

"Meg," Liz blurted out.

Mama put her hand on Liz's shoulder. "Now hear me out. You know your cousin is not a happy woman. I think we should try to teach her to do for others— about Christian charity."

"I can't influence my cousin. I pray for her, but I have no idea how to talk to her."

" 'Be kindly affectioned one to another with brotherly love; in honour preferring one another,' " her mother said, quoting from Romans.

Liz sighed. "I will try, Mother, but I teach reading and writing. I don't do miracles."

"I have an idea. Could Meg help with the Christmas pageant?"

"I've been thinking about having some of the children read the Christmas story while the others act it out. I could ask Meg to help when they forget their verses," Liz suggested thoughtfully.

Matthew had just come into the kitchen. "Couldn't you just give her the part of the donkey? She's as stubborn as a mule, so acting like a donkey would come easy."

"Matthew!" his mother scolded. "We're trying to find a way to help Meg be a better person. We need your encouragement rather than your sarcasm."

"I'm afraid none of my ideas would offer you much help," Matthew said and retreated to the parlor with the plate of cookies he had come after.

Edie came to her mother for help threading a needle in time to hear the conversation with her brother. "Would Cousin Meg help us fill the bags for the children?" she asked innocently.

Liz jumped up to hug her sister. "You have the best ideas in the world." Kissing the top of Edie's head, she said softly, "I love you so much."

Returning to her mother's side, Liz promised, "I will call on Meg tomorrow."

"And I will pray for your success," Mama said, taking her daughter's hands in hers and raising them to her lips.

❧

The next afternoon, Meg opened the door for Liz. "What do you want?" she asked, her voice filled with suspicion.

"I thought we could visit over a cup of tea," Liz said softly.

"I'm sorry. I forgot my manners." Meg led her cousin into the parlor. "I will put the tea kettle on."

"Could we sit in the kitchen? Then I can talk to you while the water heats."

"I suppose that is the way farmers do things."

"I guess we do." Liz smiled. "I always thought it was friendly."

Reluctantly, Meg led the way to the kitchen.

While Meg got out the tea things, Liz told her about the bright red bags they were making to give the children at Christmas. "Would you like to help us fill them?" she asked.

"Why?" Meg put the teapot on the table.

"It will be fun to see the children's faces when they receive their gifts."

Absently, Meg poured the tea and handed a cup to Liz. "I've never done anything like that."

"I thought you would enjoy being part of the Christmas program at school and could hand out the gifts."

"Me?"

"Why not you? Uncle David would be proud to see you take part in the community."

"Papa is mad at me," Meg confessed, sitting down opposite Liz. "He says I am selfish."

Liz swallowed over the lump in her throat. *Meg needs love.* She reached out to put her hand over her cousin's. "Then show him you have changed. Come help me with the children."

Tears stood in Meg's eyes when she looked up. "I would like to please Papa," she admitted quietly and then smiled brightly. "Yes, I would love to help with the schoolchildren's Christmas. What are we going to put in the bags?"

thirteen

With Edwina on one side and Elizabeth on the other, Mama made her way into the church on Sunday. The girls led their mother to a seat and stood nearby.

"Look, Mama. Aunt Sally is back." Liz motioned toward the back of the church.

The smile of pleasure that lighted her mother's face brought a warm glow to Liz. "I'll go get her to sit next to you." Liz hurried to Aunt Sally's side. "Mama is right down there," Liz pointed. "Won't you come sit with her?"

The two women greeted each other with hugs and kisses. "When did you get back?" Mama asked.

"Daniel brought me in yesterday." Aunt Sally patted Mama's hand. "It is so good to be home."

"I want to hear all about that baby. Will you come to dinner with us after church?"

Sally smiled. "Fannie and Tom have invited me."

"And you want to see those adorable grandsons of yours. I understand, but will you come out soon?"

"Why don't you come spend a day with me? You could ride in with Liz some morning."

"I can't leave Edie alone all day," Mama protested.

"I wouldn't be alone, Mama. Papa will be in the barn," Edie spoke from her place near her mother.

"Let her grow up, Emily," Aunt Sally said quietly.

"Are you sure you would be all right?" Mama asked.

Liz watched her shy sister lift her chin and announce, "I am not a child. I will be just fine by myself." With a start, Liz realized Edie was correct. At nearly sixteen, she now did most all the household chores. *She can read a little bit and do some arithmetic,*

Liz acknowledged. *That's as much as many women on the frontier can do. Edwina doesn't need someone to take care of her.* The thought shocked Liz. *Does this mean someday I could be free to have a family of my own?*

As Pastor Ames stood up to lead the first hymn, Liz tried to push such thoughts to the back of her mind. But looking at Pastor Ames and thinking of having her own family sent waves of disturbing feelings tumbling through her.

❧

On Wednesday, Mama got up early. Liz helped her dress, and Father lifted her into the buggy.

"Don't worry, Emily. I will be mending some harness in the barn. Edie is not alone," he said, giving her a final kiss on her cheek.

As she lifted the reins, Liz felt her mother sigh. Edie came running from the house. "You forgot your lunch, Liz." The girl handed up a bundle for her sister.

Liz smiled and thanked her sister before turning to her mother. "I'm the one who needs looking after in this household!"

When a bit later Liz pulled the horse to a stop in Aunt Sally's yard, Pastor Ames hurried out the back door. "Let me lift you down, Emily."

"All this attention will go to my head."

As Liz noticed how her mother tried to hide the pain of getting down to the ground, she shook her head in admiration. Her mother was one of the most courageous people she knew.

"Welcome," Aunt Sally called from the back door. "Come into the kitchen. I just took cinnamon rolls out of the oven."

"I'll never refuse one of Sally Miller's cinnamon rolls," Pastor said as he helped Mama up the back steps. "Can you stay for awhile, Liz?" he asked.

"I need to get to school. The children will be waiting for me." She smiled at Aunt Sally. "But you could save one of those rolls for me."

❧

When the two women were safely seated in the kitchen, Pastor followed Liz to help unhitch her horse.

"He cares for her," Sally said wistfully.

Emily nodded her head. "First we have to convince Meg she doesn't have first choice."

Sally shook her head. "When is the last time anyone convinced Meg of anything? I heard from Fannie that Meg is organizing the Christmas pageant for the school."

Emily sighed and picked up her teacup. "I suggested we try to get Meg involved in helping others. As a start, I asked Liz to invite Meg take part in the Christmas pageant."

"And now she says she is running it." Sally sighed and broke off a piece of cinnamon roll.

"It's a start, Sally. If the girl will find out she gets attention from doing good, she may start to change."

"And you don't see how devious she is? Already she is taking credit for Liz's work."

"We have to start somewhere."

"Well, apparently Pastor is trying get Meg more interested in church activities. He is starting a new Bible study class. He even asked Meg to hold the meetings at her house. Can you guess what they are studying?"

"I am sure you will tell me," Emily said and giggled.

"Matthew five."

"The Beatitudes? Meg is not going to like hearing that acts of righteousness should be done quietly." Thoughtfully Emily took a bite of roll. "Then again, if she sees the rewards given for kindness, she may move on to better behavior." Emily sighed. "I guess Pastor has chosen a good place to start."

"This is going to take a lot of prayers."

"Amen," Emily said, holding her cup out for a refill.

❧

"Are you warm enough?" Liz asked her mother on the way home that afternoon.

"I'm fine, but it is getting nippy. Your father is going to want to butcher hogs soon."

"I do not like that mess."

"I don't either," Mama admitted.

Liz reached over to pat her mother's arm. "At lease there won't be wolves to scare us," she said, referring to years earlier when the smell of butchering would lure wolves close to the house.

"We'll have a lot of work to salt the pork." Mama sighed. "We'll melt the hog fat in the big washtub as usual to make lard. With the extra fat, we should make soap."

Liz knew her mother fretted at not being able to do more of the work herself. "Edie will do whatever you tell her. Did you ask Aunt Sally to come help?"

Mama shook her head. "No, but I'm sure she will come if we ask her."

Liz giggled. "And she will tell us about leaching lye out of the wood ashes to make soap years ago."

"I'll ask your father to go by the asherie and buy some lye."

"We could buy soap from Uncle David instead of going to all the work of making our own," Liz suggested.

"We'll buy some of the refined soap for bathing," her mother agreed, "but you know we need the lye soap to wash clothes and dishes."

"I will come home from school as early as I can to help."

"Matthew will stay home from building the school, and your father will hire Rufus Wheeler's boys to help."

"They should be in school," Liz protested.

"By next year they'll be working full time as farmers and not bothering with learning sums."

"Then why are we building a fancy new school?" Liz asked in frustration.

"Now you know only a few students will be able to go on to higher-level classes. The small schools like yours teach them to read and write. Most will make their livelihood like your father. They will work the land. And for them, knowing how to read, write, and compute basic sums will suffice. Very few children will go on to teach or take jobs in town."

"Pastor Ames went on to school," Liz said quietly.

"Do you miss having him at the house every evening?"

Liz couldn't speak. The torment of having the pastor part of her family night after night had been agony. She felt her mother looking at her. "He is nice, and Edie likes to have him as a guest for supper," Liz managed to say lamely.

"Sally says he is starting a new Bible study group. Would you like to attend?"

Liz sighed. "I'm busy with school and helping at home. I'll make do with listening to Papa read the Bible before we go to bed at night." She glanced at her mother and then did a double take. Had that been a knowing smile she'd seen Mama give?

❧

Stephen Ames stopped by the brick works south of town. "Wanted to see the process," he explained to one of the workman.

"Well, the clay is dug from the creek bed and hauled here." The man pointed to the oxen treading around a pit. "The animals' hooves mix it for us to form into bricks."

Watching the process, Stephen was startled by a slap on the back and a hearty, "Come to help build the school?"

Turning, he offered his hand to John Howard. "I am told it is your determination that has the school building going up."

Mr. Howard laughed. "You took so many of my workers to build your church last summer, we are way behind in getting the bricks laid." He looked at the gray, cold sky and commented, "Getting cold for the mortar to set."

"Sorry if I caused you grief. Now our church members are helping with the school. I came to see if I could work too."

"You're more than welcome. And when we're finished, as I've promised, you can have your meetings on the first floor until you have a place of your own."

"You've mentioned a first floor before. Do you plan to build a second?"

"I do. I must admit I'm not getting much support, but I will find the funds somehow. We need the first floor for meetings, a courtroom, and primary classes. The second floor will house a high school. We will grow into more than a farm community, and when that day comes, we'll need a better school system."

"I admire your dream. Educating our youth is important," Stephen said. "Where do I sign up to work?"

"Just show up at dawn and join the crew. We try to pay a small amount to the workers. Because so many are farmers and are busy with crops, it's the only way we can coax them to work here."

"How long have you been building?"

"Well, the commissioners voted for consolidation and a high school a few years ago. Most of the subscriptions have been paid in labor and materials. We hope to finish so we can start classes in the new building next year."

"I look forward to doing my part." Stephen bid John Howard good-bye.

Arriving at the site early the next morning, Stephen joined the men hauling bricks and mixing mortar.

"Mighty cold. These walls will not set proper if they get frozen," the crew boss fretted.

Stephen looked around. The walls were up, but no floor had been laid. He could see the sky above, as the shingles would go on last. "Could we start a fire?" he suggested.

"Hmmm." The boss appeared to be considering his idea. Then he turned to Stephen. "You got a good idea there, Pastor Ames. I'll get some men started cutting brush."

As the word spread of the plan for a fire, workers offered to bring logs from their farms to add to the growing stack of wood.

"Have to keep this burning all night," the crew boss told his workers.

"I'll be happy to stay for part of the night," Stephen offered.

Other voices spoke up to volunteer their services as well.

"I need to go home for a wagon load of logs," Matthew said. "But when I come back, I can stay the night."

Soon a schedule was drawn up, and the fires began burning inside the walls of the school building. Stephen helped pile the brush high and watched to keep the fire going.

A couple hours later as Matthew drove his wagon up next to the pile of brush and wood, he said apologetically, "Sorry to be late getting back. My sisters made me wait while they finished up frying some doughnuts for you."

"Good timing, Matthew. I just went home and made coffee," his cousin Phillip called, hauling a large metal pot from his wagon.

The men gathered around the heat of the fire and enjoyed the coffee and doughnuts.

Liz would be the one to remember the workers and send food, Stephen thought. *She's stayed up late cooking and will be at school early to teach.* He sighed. If only he could find a way to break through those barriers she had so competently built between them.

fourteen

Liz looked up from her work as Meg entered the kitchen of the Miller farmhouse. Wrapped in a bright blue cloak, her hair done to perfection, and her head held high, Meg walked gracefully to greet Mama.

"I came to help," Meg announced, bending to blow a kiss in the direction of her aunt's cheek.

Mama smiled at her niece. "It was Edie's idea to make gingerbread men to put in the children's Christmas surprise packages."

Meg's eyebrows lifted as she gave Edwina a skeptical glance.

"Mama told me how to mix the batter," Edie said proudly.

"I have never made cookies," Meg admitted, taking off her cloak.

Liz took the garment and hung it on a peg. Silently she prayed Meg would not hurt her sister's feelings.

"That's a lovely dress," Mama complimented Meg. "Liz, will you get an apron for your cousin? It wouldn't do for her to get spots on her nice outfit."

Without a word, she did her mother's bidding and helped Meg pin an apron over her pretty dress.

"You'll have to tell me how I can help." Meg's tone held a note of apprehension

"Edie is the cook around here," Liz said. "She will show you what to do. I'm sure you will find it fun."

"Really?" Meg seemed to avoid looking at Edie, who stood eager to please.

"I can roll out the dough, and you can cut the gingerbread men," Edie offered.

Liz stood by her mother's side, and Mama smiled up at her with reassurance.

Meg followed Edie to the table and watched while the girl

rolled out the spicy dough. Her look of uneasiness made Liz wonder if they had made a mistake in inviting Meg to help.

Edie picked up the cookie cutter. "You dip it in a little flour and then cut out the gingerbread men." Turning to her mother, the girl asked, "Should we put the eyes and buttons on before we bake them?"

"That's right, Dear."

"Eyes? Buttons? I can't sew either," Meg protested.

Edie giggled. Picking up a small bowl nearby, she showed her cousin. "We use dried elderberries and dried currents for eyes and buttons. Watch, I'll show you."

"I can do that," Meg stated firmly, looking a little relieved.

"Then let's get started." Edie went back to rolling out dough.

Liz got down the teapot and started a pot to steep. "The oven is hot, Edie. Do you want me to put in the cookies that are ready to bake?"

"Yes, please," Edie replied.

Meg bent over the table, pushing currents down the front of the little figures she had cut out. "Oh, I pushed too hard," she moaned.

"That's all right," Mama said. "We all make our share of mistakes on projects like these."

The girls worked in the warm kitchen. Liz piled more wood in the stove to keep the oven hot. Pulling another pan of cookies out of the oven, she slid them onto the counter by the sink. "We have made a mess of the kitchen," she apologized to her mother.

Smiling, Mama sniffed the air. "I do love the smell of gingerbread baking. Why don't you girls take a break and enjoy some of the fresh cookies and tea?"

Meg turned from the table and pushed a stray hair off her face, leaving a streak of flour.

She is pretty when she relaxes, Liz realized. She looked at her cousin, who stood so tall next to tiny Edie. Both girls had the brown curls from their mothers' side of the family. Pleasure filled Liz as she watched Meg put a hand on Edie's shoulder. "You do good work," Meg said. "I guess I should learn to cook."

"I could teach you," Edie offered willingly. Then the girl looked at her mother. "But we would need Mama to tell us what to do."

Liz handed her mother a cup of tea. Mama smiled wistfully. "You look just like your mother, Meg. Brings back good memories of when we baked together." She laughed. "You were little then and sat on the table sprinkling sugar on the cookies we baked for Christmas."

Meg looked sad. "I don't remember much about my mother."

"She loved you dearly."

Meg took the cup of tea Liz offered her and came to sit on the stool at Mama's feet. "I like to hear you talk about her."

Edie carried a plate of broken pieces to the women. "We have to eat the mistakes," she said, popping a bite of gingerbread into her mouth.

Later, when the finished cookies cooled on the table, Meg looked out the window. "Oh, it's starting to get dark. The day has gone by so quickly, I did not watch the time."

"Will you come help us fill the children's bags before the pageant?" Liz asked.

"I would like that." Meg sounded surprised at her own acceptance. Stammering, she added, "I've had a good time today." She walked to Edie and gave the girl a hug. "I've gotten to know my other cousin," she said sincerely.

Liz sighed and silently thanked God for watching over her sister. "Edie is a big help."

"She has been such a blessing to me since I hurt my back," Mama added, reaching up to pat Meg's face when the girl bent to plant a kiss on her cheek.

"I hope you will come again soon," Edie said softly.

Meg did come back a few days later to help fill the bags. She brought hard candy to add to the treats in the packages. "Papa said since I was good about not getting a new dress for Christmas, I could have candy from the store."

"Your dress looks new," Mama said when Meg hung her cloak on a peg.

"Mrs. Greely put new lace and ribbons on the collar." She looked almost shy when she bent down to kiss her aunt. "I wore it to show you."

"I am honored." Mama patted Meg's hand.

"How is the program coming?" Meg asked Liz.

"The children know their verses, but I'm sure they will forget them when they have to stand in front of all the people. We will really need you to prompt them."

Liz looked at her cousin and noticed Meg's eyes light up with joy at the idea of being needed by others. For the first time, she had hope that Meg might change for the better after all.

❧

The weather turned cold and frosty the Sunday afternoon of the pageant. "At least the snow held off," Father said as he lifted Mama into the wagon. "Are you sure you will be warm enough?" he asked her.

"I'm fine. Do the girls have the box of presents for the children?"

"First thing that went into the wagon. Edie saw to that." Father chuckled as he helped the girls into the back of the wagon with Matthew.

When the Millers arrived at the schoolhouse, Liz hurried ahead of her family to meet the children. Excited students crowded around her. She tried to get them lined up in order.

"What can I do?" Meg asked.

Liz turned to see Meg in her fancy dress with her hair fixed in curls at the nape of her neck. Absently Liz patted the simple bun on the back of her head.

"Are you ready?" Pastor asked over the clamor of the milling children.

Liz smiled. "As ready as we will ever be." She turned to Meg. "Why don't you stand at the side where the children can hear you if you have to help them?"

The program started with Pastor Ames leading the singing. Then Liz coaxed one child after another to come forward and repeat a verse of the Christmas story. Proud parents and grandparents listened respectfully as the age-old story unfolded.

When the oldest children had come forward to sing "Shout the Glad Tidings," Pastor made his way to the front of the schoolroom. At the end of the song, he urged the youngsters to stay where they were. "We have one more part to the program. Miss Elizabeth, Miss Margaret, and Miss Edwina have been busy preparing a surprise for all the children," he announced to the congregation. "I would like those ladies to come forward and let us thank them for their labors."

Liz looked for Edie, who seemed to shrink behind their mother. Her dilemma was solved when Pastor went to the girl and offered her his arm and escorted her forward to join her sister and cousin. Everyone stood to applaud. "Now," Pastor announced, "I want all the children to line up to come get your Christmas surprise."

Edwina ducked back behind the teacher's desk where the box of treats had been hidden. "You give them out," she begged her sister.

"Meg, will you help me?" Liz asked. "Edie and I will hand you the bags, and you can give them to the children."

Meg didn't need a second invitation. As the children came up and each received a red bag tied with green yarn, they thanked her and ran back to their parents to see what was tucked inside.

Jamie held his little brother George's hand until they stood in front of Meg. George took his bag and promptly bit the head off the gingerbread man sticking out of the top. Jamie reached up to give Meg a kiss on the cheek. Liz turned in time to see the look of joy that crossed Meg's face.

Thank You, Lord. Meg is getting the idea of how good it feels to give, Liz prayed as she continued to hand Meg bags of cookies, apples, and candy for the excited children.

"Did we have enough bags?" Edie asked on the way home.

"There were some left, and Meg offered to take them to children who were not there today."

"Meg did that?" Matthew asked in surprise. "What a change. She acts almost nice."

"We hope it's a new beginning for her," his mother answered.

"Will she and Uncle David and Phillip come for Christmas dinner?" Edie asked.

"We invited them, and I'm sure David will be with us," Father answered.

"Meg is not so bad. She has been nice to me the last two times she has been at the house," Edie said.

"I hope it lasts," Matthew said with skepticism.

❧

Uncle David did arrive with his son and daughter on Christmas Day. The young people listened, as they did every Christmas, to the story of their parent's first Christmas in Millersville.

"We were waiting to get a letter from my father giving us permission to marry," Mama explained. "A son of an Indian friend of your grandfather brought news that mail and supplies had been left at the Four Corners for us." She smiled at her husband. "Your father and Uncle David risked their lives to collect the packages in a blizzard."

"But the letter of consent was there," Father said. "With a wagon load of gifts from Emily's father."

"Are any of Colonel Dewey's sons still around here?" Phillip asked, referring to their grandfather's Indian friend.

"Grandsons now," his father answered. "Joshua works at the brick works when he isn't off hunting. It was his father who came to tell us about the wagon load of supplies that first Christmas."

The festivities and food lasted until past dark. "Won't you have more pie, Uncle David?" Edwina asked.

"I'll take a slice of that home for tomorrow. Too full to eat another bite now."

"Edie has fixed a whole basket of good food for us to take-home," Meg told her father. "She even offered to teach me to cook."

Uncle David raised his eyebrows. "Now that would be something. I might even be able to marry you off if you learn to cook."

"Father!" Meg protested with a laugh.

"Do I have to eat your experiments?" Phillip groaned.

"You are being mean, Cousin Phillip," Edie scolded. "We are trying to help. Mama taught me to cook, and she will help Meg learn."

Putting her arm around Edie, Meg scowled at her brother. "You need to listen to Edie, Brother. Maybe I can learn to cook like she can."

"I would be more than grateful," Uncle David said, giving Mama a kiss on the cheek. "Now we'd better get the lanterns lit and be on our way."

Mama stood in the circle of Father's arm, watching the sleigh disappear down the road.

"Looks like you have tamed your sister's child after all," Father said.

"Anything is an improvement," Matthew observed, coming back into the house.

Father turned to follow Mama and Matthew into the kitchen. "I missed having Pastor Ames with us. He seems so much a part of this family."

"He said he wanted to go with Sally to Tom and Fannie's. Abbie and Daniel were going to spend the day," Mama said quietly.

"We don't see him as often now that Sally is back," Father mused.

Mama nodded toward Liz, who was busy washing dishes. "Maybe he doesn't feel welcome."

Liz blushed on hearing her mother's words. In her efforts to keep from hurting Meg or letting down her family, had she inadvertently hurt the pastor's feelings?

fifteen

School resumed right after Christmas Day. The weather turned bitter cold. Each morning Pastor Ames continued to rise early and have a fire burning in the schoolroom stove by the time Liz arrived. The bigger boys kept the wood box full so Liz could keep a fire roaring all day.

"I will give out your lessons and then you can bring your books and slates closer to the stove if you would like," Liz told her students. She kept an extra shawl in her desk to wrap around her shoulders. More than once the shawl was wrapped around the thin shoulders of one of her younger girls. Liz knew the child came from a large family who struggled to survive. She felt good to know Uncle David and her father made sure the family had food during the winter.

A few days after Christmas, Liz stopped by Aunt Sally's before going home. "I can't stay long. The days are getting longer, but it still gets dark early and Edie worries if I am not home by dark," she called from the kitchen door.

"Come join us for tea," Aunt Sally answered from her chair by the fire in the parlor.

Liz hung her cloak on a peg in the kitchen and went to join Aunt Sally, praying her guest was not Pastor Ames. Perhaps in part because she so appreciated the things he did for her, such as starting the fire in the stove at school, she still had trouble hiding her feelings when she was close to him.

As she stepped into the parlor, her fears were relieved at the sight of her cousin. "Hello, Meg," Liz said warmly. Stopping in wonder, she blurted out, "What are you doing?"

Meg giggled. "Aunt Sally is trying to teach me to knit." She held up the beginning of a wool shawl.

"It looks nice," Liz encouraged.

"I had so much fun baking cookies with your family, I decided to try to learn some other things."

"What are you going to do with the shawl?" Liz asked, an idea forming in her head.

"You need it?" Meg laughed.

"No, but one of my students could use it."

"You think I could make something good enough to give away?"

Liz took the cup her aunt Sally offered and sat next to Meg. "Why not? This child is very thin, and she has no shawl." She smiled as she took a sip of tea. "I often put an extra one of mine around her."

"I did like giving out the Christmas surprises," Meg admitted shyly. "Father seemed very proud of me," she added quietly.

"He told me how much you reminded him of your mother when you stood up there with the children," Aunt Sally said.

"Really?" Meg held up the shawl. "You can see the mistakes," she grimaced.

"But it could keep a child warm," Liz told her cousin.

"I'll keep trying, but now I have to get home. I promised Mattie I would peel potatoes." Meg carefully put her knitting back in the bag next to her. After giving both her cousin and grandmother a kiss, she took down her cloak. "Thank you for the lesson, Aunt Sally. I'll come by again soon."

After the door closed, Aunt Sally smiled at Liz. "What do you think?"

"I think we had a miracle this Christmas. I just hope it lasts."

"Your idea to let her give the shawl to a needy child will keep her trying."

Liz drained her cup and took it to the kitchen. "Now I'd better be on my way."

"How is Emily?" Aunt Sally asked, getting up to go to the door with Liz.

"She doesn't say much, but I can see the cold weather makes her more stiff and sore. Edie keeps warm bricks close to her and the poultices on her back. Polly says there is nothing more we can do."

"I hope the town fathers find a doctor for Millersville soon. Polly's daughter Harriet is a good midwife, but we need a real doctor living here."

"Do you think he could help mother?" Liz asked eagerly.

"No, but he would be here if we have another influenza epidemic."

Liz sighed and wrapped her cloak around her. She knew Aunt Sally's first husband had died of influenza and left her with a young son and pregnant with Abbie. "I pray we do not have an outbreak of the disease. We have been fortunate for the past two years."

"Yes, we will pray both for a doctor and for no epidemic," Aunt Sally said, patting Liz on her arm. "Give my love to your mother."

❧

At supper that night, Father lamented, not the cold weather, but the lack of snow. "If we don't get a blanket of snow on the land, we won't get a good run of sap in the spring," he grumbled.

"Be patient, Dear," Mama cautioned. "The winter is young."

Liz told of her visit to Aunt Sally and how Meg was learning to knit. "She's making a shawl and will give it to the Jenkins child."

"Meg!" Matthew exclaimed. "Liz, I think you did a miracle with that one."

Liz shook her head. "Not me." She reached to pat her sister's hand. "Edie got her interested in learning to do for others." Looking at the surprised girl next to her, she told Edie, "Meg told me again today how much fun she had baking cookies with you."

Edie flushed with pleasure.

"You could teach Cousin Meg a lot, little sister," Matthew said through a mouthful of food. "Your biscuits are delicious."

"Would you like some pie?" Edie asked eagerly.

When the meal was over, Father pulled back Mama's chair. "Let the girls clean up, Emily. Come sit by the parlor stove with me."

"I'll go separate the milk," Matthew offered.

Edie dipped hot water from the pot on the back of the stove into the dishpan. As she washed the dishes and Liz dried them and put them on the shelf, Edie asked, "Liz, why don't you like Pastor Ames?"

Liz froze. The plate in her hand hung midway to the shelf. She could not speak.

Edie didn't look up from the soapy water. "You never want Mama to invite him for dinner. All the rest of us like to have him around, but you don't even want to look at him."

"I like him," Liz stammered, finally getting the plate safely in its place.

"He looks at you so sad. I think you are unkind," Edie declared, wringing out her dishcloth.

Liz stood with the dish towel in her hand, watching her sister wipe off the kitchen table. Her mind whirled. *Unkind. That's what Mama and Father seemed to be saying on Christmas evening. But what am I to do? The better I know him, the more I realize I could truly care for him. But what would Meg do if she knew I cared about the pastor? Could it keep her from continuing to change her ways?*

Matthew came through the back door, stomping his feet and rubbing his hands. He stopped and looked at Liz in puzzlement. "Are you all right? You look different."

Liz gulped and tried to straighten both her back and her thoughts.

"I asked her why she does not like Pastor Ames," Edie explained, still working on the kitchen table.

Matthew looked from one sister to the other. "You are very cold toward him, Liz," he commented. "Maybe it only seems that way because you are the only single girl in town who isn't trying to gain his attention."

"Jane is nice to him, and she's not interested in getting him to marry her," Edie countered, going back to her soapy water. She grinned at her brother. "Her new locket is very pretty."

Liz watched her brother blush and lost some of her confusion.

"I'm sorry I have been rude to the pastor. I promise to do better," Liz told her siblings in a quiet voice.

"How is the weather out there?" Father asked Matthew from the parlor door.

"I think it's a little warmer. You always say it has to warm up to snow. Could happen before morning," Matthew reported, hanging his coat on a nearby peg.

Liz went to the other room to be near her mother.

"You look troubled, Dear. Problems at school?"

"No. A scolding from Edie," Liz said, pulling a footstool close to her mother and sitting down.

Mama patted Liz's head and smiled. "What could that sweet child find to scold about?"

Liz looked into her mother's soft brown eyes. "She thinks I am unkind to Pastor Ames."

Mama sighed. "You seem very distant from him. Are you afraid of him for some reason?"

Liz swallowed hard. "No," she whispered. "I am afraid of myself."

"He cares for you, you know," her mother told her, brushing a stray strand of hair back from her daughter's face.

Fear swept through Liz. "No, no." She shook her head. "That cannot be."

"You certainly have not encouraged him, but when he looks at you, I can see the longing in his eyes. Is there a reason you do not care for him?"

"But I do," Liz blurted out as the tears pressed against her eyelids.

"Meg," Mama said softly. "You have stayed back because of Meg, haven't you?"

Liz tried to brush the tears back as she looked up and murmured, "Yes."

"Liz, you cannot make the pastor prefer your cousin over you. What God has ordained will be. If Pastor Ames is in love with you and you could love him, it is because God wills it."

"But what of Meg? She's just beginning to change."

"She has caused her own problems, and you are helping her. But it won't help her to think she can marry the wrong man." Mama pulled a handkerchief from her pocket and dabbed her daughter's cheeks. "And it wouldn't hurt for you to smile at Pastor once in awhile."

Liz put her head in her mother's lap. "I have been so scared. I didn't even dare look at him. What must he think of me?"

"Let's invite him for supper and see. Edie loves to cook for him. Your whole family likes to have him around. He is a God-fearing man, Liz. Trust him to do the right thing."

❧

The promised snow fell. Liz could not get to school for two days. Finally the drifts were shoveled back so her sleigh could make the trip. When she got to Aunt Sally's home, Pastor Ames stood in the barn, waiting for her.

"Have you been going to the school every day?" she asked him.

"No. I knew you wouldn't be able to get to town. I did check to make sure no children came in and were left alone."

"Thank you," she said, daring to look him in the face. *He is a gentle, kind man of faith. I really do care for him.*

"Come in and get warm before you go to school," Aunt Sally called from the kitchen door.

"There is a fire going and the door is open for any children who come early," Pastor said, offering his arm for her to hold on to and guiding her to the house.

When he put his hand over hers, Liz felt a warm glow. Quietly she stepped into Aunt Sally's house and away from Pastor Ames. "I will have a quick cup of coffee, but I must get to school."

Sitting at the table with her cloak thrown back over the chair, Liz listened to Aunt Sally talk about the snow and how the town had managed to deal with the storm.

"Father is pleased," Liz reported. "He says the fields need a blanket to keep them warm for the winter." She took a sip of the hot coffee. Looking over the rim of the cup to Pastor, she realized he sat watching her. "My sister wants you to come for supper soon," she told him.

"Only your sister?"

Liz felt herself blush and bowed her head to hide it. "No, my whole family misses you and would like you to come out for a meal."

"You tell Edie I look forward to one of her meals, and I will come for supper on Wednesday if that is all right."

"I'm sure it will be. Now I must be on my way. Thank you for the coffee, Aunt Sally." She bent to kiss the woman's wrinkled cheek.

"You give Emily my love. I will come out to see her when there is a break in the weather."

❧

Wednesday arrived. Liz had as much trouble as her students paying attention to lessons. *Pastor Ames has been to your house dozens of times,* she thought. *But not since Mother said he loved you,* she reminded herself. *Could it be true?*

Liz hurried home after school. "I came to see if I could help," she called to her sister as she hung up her cloak.

"It's just Pastor coming to supper. Why would I need help?" Edie asked. "I did bake a cake this afternoon. Do you think he will like it?"

"I'm certain he'll like anything you fix." Liz hugged her sister. "I can't believe how much you've grown up. You used to be my baby sister. Now you cook and clean better than I do." Liz walked to her mother's chair and bent to give her a kiss. "Did you have a good day?" she asked as Mama put her knitting needles down.

"Every day the Lord gives me is fine," her mother answered.

The last-minute supper preparations kept Liz too busy to worry about the pastor's arrival, that is, until she heard the sound of his horse trotting toward the barn. She stood back when Pastor Ames reached the front door.

Liz's father and brother greeted their guest enthusiastically. The pastor shook their hands and then walked over to her mother. "Nice of you to invite me," he told her.

Mama smiled and nodded at Liz when Pastor went to speak to Edie. "Supper is ready," the girl told them.

Liz helped her sister serve up pot roast, potatoes, carrots, corn bread, and applesauce. "I made cake for dessert," Edie announced when everyone had eaten their fill of the food in front of them.

"We are full, Dear," her father said. "You girls clean up the dishes and we will have coffee and cake later."

"Let me help," Pastor said, starting to pile plates to be washed.

Liz watched him banter with her sister. He didn't seem to notice her as she covered the food and took it to the back storeroom to stay cold. *Mother must be wrong,"* Liz concluded. *He's completely indifferent to me.*

"Let me get the door for you," Pastor said as she balanced a plate of leftover meat.

Liz looked into the pastor's face. She could see herself reflected in his shining dark eyes. Her heart beat in her throat, making speech impossible. Absently, she put the platter on a shelf without taking her gaze away from him.

Neither spoke. No words were necessary to express the feelings passing between them. And in that moment, Liz knew that the pastor was anything but indifferent to her presence.

sixteen

Liz walked to the school from Aunt Sally's to start another day of teaching. Her emotions warred within her. After months of hiding her feelings, she could not find a way to express herself openly.

Am I dreaming? Could Pastor Ames really care for me? Her thoughts raced forward to envision a life beside him. *Am I good enough to be a pastor's wife?*

An insistent voice broke into her thoughts. "Miss Elizabeth, Miss Elizabeth, my papa says the creek is frozen enough so we can go skating. Will you skate with us on Saturday?"

Jamie bounced up and down in front of her. Absently touching his copper curls, Liz remembered the many pairs of skates her grandpa George had carved out of wood. The double runners that he'd given her had strapped to her shoes, and she'd felt she could fly on the ice. "Do you still have the skates Grandpa carved?"

The eager child bobbed his head up and down. "My papa says they are the ones Grandpa carved for him. Do you have yours?"

Liz smiled. "Yes, but they are too small now." Then she laughed. "Maybe they would fit my sister."

"Can she come too? She is fun. Edwina is little like me, but she is really a grown-up."

"I never thought of her like that." Liz pictured her four-foot, eight-inch sister and realized she was not much taller than Jamie. "I'll tell her you invited her to skate."

Jamie bounced off to invite others to come to the creek to skate on Saturday. Liz could hear his excited voice as the children prepared to go home after the school day. She made a mental note to encourage Edwina to join in the fun. Considering how many public activities her sister had taken part in over the past few months, she might be willing to try skating now, although she had always turned offers down in the past.

But when Liz passed on the invitation to Edie that evening, the girl frowned. "Liz, I limp. How could I skate?"

"The same way you walk, little sister," Matthew told her with a quick hug. "Come with us. I will ask Jane, and we will be there to help you up if you fall."

"Will you skate?" Edie asked her brother with wonder in her voice.

He laughed. "I don't have skates big enough, but I will keep a bonfire going so you can get warm."

"Do we have any chocolate, Edie?" Mama asked. "You could invite people to come back here for hot chocolate."

"I can buy some more at Uncle David's mercantile if we need it," Liz offered.

"Sounds like a good time," Father said. "But when do I get fed tonight?"

"Oh. I have it all ready. Sit down, and I will put your supper on the table." Edie scurried to feed her father as fast as she could.

❧

Saturday dawned bright, cold, and beautiful. "Let's take the wagon, Emily," Father suggested as Liz made sure Edie had her skates. "You can visit Sally while the children are off having a good time."

"What will you do?" Mama asked.

"I will enjoy a cup of coffee with you and Sally and then I will go visit David. I want to find out if he has heard any more about getting a doctor to settle in Millersville."

"We do need someone closer than Prattsville," Mama agreed.

With the excitement of getting Edie to join in the skating, Liz had not thought of Pastor Ames until she put on her cloak. *What if he comes to the creek? Do I dare talk to him?*

"Come on, Liz. We're ready to leave," her brother called from the back door.

"Is Jane coming?" Edie asked Matthew.

"She'll meet us there. She's bringing her little sister to join the others."

"You think you have wood enough?" Father asked.

"Others are bringing wood too," Matthew answered.

"Sounds like a good time." Mama sighed. Liz cringed as her mother tried to shift in a vain effort to ease the pain in her back.

Jonathan dropped the children off at the spot where Black Creek spread out shallow and wide. The ice formed thick and safe in that area, unlike around the bridge. There the creek ran swift and deep before tumbling into the field by the new school building.

"I will leave the wagon at Aunt Sally's, Matthew. You can come get it when you are ready to go home," Father explained as he got ready to go.

"That will be fine, Pa. We'll tuck Mother in snug and stop by Uncle David's to pick you up on the way home."

Edie clung to Liz as they approached a group of people already skating on the ice.

"I don't think I can do this," Edie whimpered.

Liz put a protective arm around her sister. "They have a fire going over on the bank. Let's go stand by it and watch for awhile. When you feel ready to try, remember Matthew promised that he and Jane would go with you, so you don't have to go out there by yourself."

❧

Stephen Ames approached the young people gathered by the cleared ice. He watched some who skated well and others who managed to stay upright by flapping their arms. His breath caught in his throat when he saw Liz. He could read the concern in her face as she spoke to her sister. The hood of her cloak hid her beautiful hair, but he well remembered what it looked like.

She fills my dreams. Did I imagine her response to me? Did she really look at me with love? Dear Lord, it is my greatest wish to have her by my side. We could serve You well if it is Your will.

"Hello, Pastor. Did you come to skate?" Matthew asked as he extended his gloved hand to Stephen in greeting.

"I came to watch. I don't have skates, and if I did, I doubt I could remember how to use them," Stephen joked as he shook Matthew's hand.

"Come join us at the fire. No need to freeze while we talk."

Stephen walked with Matthew to where Liz and Edie stood. "Aren't you going to give it a try, Edie?" Matthew asked his sister.

Stephen thought of a frightened deer when he looked into Edie's eyes. Immediately he reached out to her. "Let me help you. I'll strap your skates on and then walk with you on the ice."

Edie looked from Liz to the pastor. Liz nodded her head, and Stephen saw her grateful expression. "Pastor Ames will take care of you," she told the girl.

I would gladly take care of you the rest of my life, Stephen thought, looking at Liz. He took the skates in Edie's hand. "Come sit here." He motioned to a seat carved in the snow bank. "We will have you floating on the ice in no time."

"I hope I am on my feet when I do that floating," Edie said, then giggled nervously.

Stephen gently pulled Edie to her feet, holding her arms so she would not fall. "Cross your arms over mine and hold on. We won't go fast, so you will just slide over the ice on the skates."

Liz stood back, holding her breath. *Please, Lord. Don't let her get hurt.*

Slowly Edie appeared to gain confidence. Pastor pulled her faster and faster. Liz felt tears fill her eyes at the joy she read in her sister's face. Just then, the pastor looked at her and waved. Liz wiped the tears from her cheeks and self-consciously waved back.

"Remember when Grandpa made us skates?"

Liz turned to see Meg. "Yes. The skates Edie is wearing are the ones he made me."

"She looks so happy. Pastor will be worn out pulling her," Meg said with a laugh.

"He is very kind and compassionate with her," Liz said quietly, hoping her voice did not betray her feelings.

"He's good to everyone. We are lucky to have such a fine pastor.

I wish you would come to the Bible study he holds at our house each week," Meg invited.

"Perhaps I will try," Liz murmured, knowing she could never sit in the same room with him and hide her feelings from Meg and the others. Liz looked at her cousin. Meg watched the skaters, but she didn't seem to dwell on Pastor Ames. Was it possible she was losing interest in him?

"We were planning on having hot chocolate at our house after the skating," Liz told her cousin. "Would you like to come?"

"Why don't we all go to my house? It's closer," Meg suggested. Then she laughed. "I'll have to ask Edie to make the hot chocolate. I'd probably burn it."

Liz smiled. "Matthew is supposed to go to Aunt Sally's to get our wagon and pick up Mother and then go to your house to fetch Father. We could all meet Matthew there."

"I'll go talk to Matthew and Jane and tell them of our plans," Meg said, hurrying off.

Just as Meg left, Edie stopped in a swirl in front of her sister. "I'm really skating. I can skate without a limp," she exclaimed.

Liz looked from her sister's rosy cheeks and big smile to Pastor Ames. He still kept a steadying hand on Edie's back. "Thank you," she told him. His answering smile dazzled her.

"Are you warm enough, Edie?" Liz asked in concern.

"You're the one standing on the ice," Edie fussed. "I think your feet must be cold."

Liz smiled. "A little bit. When you have had enough here, Meg has invited us to come have hot chocolate." Then Liz laughed. "But she says you have to make it because she would only burn it."

"I thought we were going home for hot chocolate."

"It's closer to go to Uncle David's, and we have to stop there for Father anyway."

"Will you come too?" Edie asked Pastor eagerly.

Liz met his questioning look and nodded her head.

Edie went out on the ice alone for a short time before she

came breathlessly back to her sister. "I didn't fall down." As she started to teeter, Pastor Ames reached out to catch her. The radiant girl giggled and got her balance again. "I better stop while I'm still in one piece."

"Let me help you take the skates off." Pastor helped Edie to the same seat as before and unstrapped her skates. Standing, he handed them to Edie and then turned to face Liz. "I'll tell Matthew you are leaving and then meet you at Meg's."

His look made Liz forget her cold feet.

❧

Liz was glad to see that Edie's excitement didn't wane. She continued to chatter all the way to their cousins' home. Stopping before they went up the steps to the house, Edie turned to her sister. "Thank you for taking me. I had such a good time."

Liz hugged her sister. "It's so wonderful to have you willing to go out. People love you and want you around. Hiding at home is not the way to live, Edie."

"You and Pastor have taught me that."

The door opened. "Come in and get warm," Uncle David invited them.

"Papa, Papa, I skated," Edwina cried as she rushed to her father.

He looked surprised and pleased at his daughter's exuberance.

"Now I have to ask her to work," Meg apologized from the kitchen door. "I invited people to have hot chocolate if Edie would make it."

Liz saw the amazed look on her uncle's face. She put her hand on his arm. "Your daughter is doing fine," she whispered.

"You were a big help in getting her started on the right path," he said in a choked voice.

"The thanks belong to the Lord. He has guided us," Liz said as they heard more footsteps on the front porch.

People gathered around the fireplace to warm hands and feet after being in the cold air by the creek. Meg was busy handing out cups of hot chocolate by the time Matthew carried his mother from the wagon into the parlor.

"What a nice party, David," she told her brother-in-law. "I thought people would come to our house."

"It's closer to come here, Aunt Emily," Meg said, offering her a cup of hot chocolate.

"Mama, I skated," Edie announced as she knelt by her mother's chair. "Pastor Ames held my hands and pulled me on the ice."

"And then she came here and made the hot chocolate," Meg added.

Liz watched the scene in wonder. Meg continued to circulate among the guests, but she didn't spend much time with the pastor. In fact, she seemed not to be seeking him out, and often she appeared unaware of his whereabouts. Liz wondered if Meg had finally given up on attracting the pastor and might be ready to accept the idea of Liz herself being interested in him.

As if he sensed her thoughts, Pastor Ames stepped close to Liz. Shyly, she looked up at him.

"So, David," Mama asked from her seat by Liz, "what is the word on a doctor coming here?"

"I believe we have one lined up." Uncle David looked at Meg. "I hope you won't mind, Dear, but I invited him to visit us this spring to see what he thinks of Millersville."

"A doctor stay here?" Meg looked stricken.

"Just for a short time. I'm sure if he decides to stay, he will quickly find a place of his own."

"Edie, you have to teach me to cook," Meg pleaded.

"Well, if your cooking makes him sick, I'm sure a doctor will know what to do," Matthew teased.

"That's not nice, Matthew," Edie protested.

Liz ignored the banter between her siblings and turned to Pastor Ames.

"Whom do you have coming?" he asked Uncle David.

"Dr. Brewster in Prattsville has a nephew graduating from Dartmouth this spring. He says the young man will move here."

"Getting dark, family. Time we headed for home," Father interrupted.

The Millers quickly put on their wraps and snuggled closely to one another in the wagon to stay warm.

"Did you have a good visit?" Liz asked her mother when they got home.

"Yes, it was nice to get out, but I'm afraid I'm all tired out."

"Let me bring you a bowl of hot soup and then we'll get you to bed." Liz nodded toward her sister. "Edie will be asleep on her feet if we wait much longer to serve supper."

❧

A foot of snow fell on Sunday night, but Liz had no trouble using the sleigh to get to school the next morning. By that afternoon, the sun shone brightly, so she stopped to visit briefly with Aunt Sally before going home.

Aunt Sally poured tea. The two women sat in the warm kitchen, and she put a plate of cookies on the table between them. "My boarder is looking very happy these days. Do you know something about this?" she asked quietly.

"My mother has been talking," Liz growled.

"Anyone with eyes can see how Pastor Ames feels. It's about time you woke up."

Liz put her cup down. "What am I going to do? Meg is just getting turned around, and I'm not sure that she's lost interest in the pastor. If I upset her now, there is no telling what she will do."

"Don't you think Meg can see how Pastor looks at you?"

Liz looked up in horror. "No. That's not possible."

"Just you trust the Lord to work things out. I think Meg is busy trying to gain her father's attention in good ways and she isn't worried about capturing Pastor Ames anymore."

"I'm so confused," Liz admitted, toying with a cookie. "But I'm very proud of my sister. She's growing up." Putting the cookie on her saucer, she continued. "Do you think she could accept my moving to a home of my own?"

"You worry too much," Aunt Sally admonished. "Let go, and let wonderful things happen."

Liz ended her visit a short time later. "I have to be home before dark," she explained, giving Aunt Sally a kiss good-bye.

The horse plodded the familiar path down Main Street. Lost in her thoughts, Liz didn't notice when they approached the bridge over Black Creek. Uncle David's house sat in the curve of the creek, but she had traveled this way so often, Liz didn't look up.

But as the horse stepped on the bridge, a woman's scream rent the air.

seventeen

Instinctively, Liz pulled back on the reins. The mare stopped partway onto the bridge. Liz heard a woman calling from the creek bank. She urged the horse across the bridge where she could turn around and go back to whomever called. Two men ran from the new school building. She recognized them as men who worked part-time for her father.

"What happened? Are you all right?" Ezra approached her followed by Clyde.

"I don't know. I heard a scream and then a woman calling from the creek. I had to turn my horse around so I could go back. Do you want a ride?"

Both men crowded onto the seat of the sleigh. As soon as they settled, Liz turned the horse and started back across the bridge. Other people were hurrying to the area. As the sleigh went over the center of the bridge, Ezra, who sat on the side where the cries had come from, said, "Looks like a break in the ice. Someone has gone through. Whoever went in the water has been swept under the ice and downstream by now."

"My cousin lives there." Liz pulled into the path to her uncle David's barn. Jumping down, she called to the men, "I have to make sure Meg is all right."

"I'll take care of your horse, Miss Elizabeth," Ezra called after her.

Liz spied her cousin and ran to where she stood in the snow. *She should have a shawl or cloak on,* Liz thought. Then she saw the stricken look on Meg's face.

"What is it? What has happened?" she demanded of her cousin.

Meg shook her head. Liz put her arms around the woman. "Are you all right, Meg? Did you fall?"

Meg only moaned. Liz turned toward the other people gathered at the creek to see what they were looking at. She saw men on the other side following the path. Then she noticed the footprints that led off the path to the ice. "Who went through, Meg?" Liz asked in a whisper.

"I killed him," came the strangled answer.

"What?" Liz exclaimed. She tightened her grip on Meg's shoulders. "Please tell me what happened." Liz knew there was no way her cousin could have pushed anyone. The footprints were on the other side of the creek. She tried to share her cloak with Meg. "You need to go back to the house before you catch cold."

Meg shuddered and stepped back from her cousin. "Have they found him?" she asked, looking toward the creek.

"Who are they looking for, Meg? Can't you tell me what you saw?"

Meg's look of agony twisted Liz's heart. She put her arm around her cousin. "Come with me. We'll go back to the house."

Shaking her head, Meg refused to move. Desperate, Liz looked around for help. Spotting Mattie, she beckoned to the woman. "Why don't you have a cloak around you?" she asked Mattie, who hurried to answer her call. "You and Meg will be chilled to the bone."

"She ran out without even a shawl. When I heard her scream, I followed her," the woman explained.

Still trying to hold Meg and keep her cloak around both of them, Liz asked Mattie, "Can you tell me what happened? Who has gone through the ice?

Liz saw Mattie look toward the creek. Men still walked up and down the sides, but with the opening in the center bubbling up cold, threatening water, no one dared to venture onto the ice.

"We were baking cookies," Mattie said in a soft voice. "Miss Margaret stood at the sink and looked out the window. She called to me that she would meet her friend on the bridge and give him some cookies. With that, she grabbed a few cookies from where they were cooling and ran out of the house."

"Who, Mattie? Who did she see?" Liz held her breath. Could that friend be Stephen Ames?

"Jamie," came the strangled cry.

Shocked, Liz watched the tears stream down the older woman's face. "Jamie?" Her voice quavered.

Mattie nodded her head. "I heard Miss Margaret scream and ran to see what had happened. She stood at the edge of the creek, but I held her back. She wanted to run out on the ice where he had gone through."

Meg continued to stand rigid in Liz's arms. "Let's get her into the house. She cannot stay out here in the cold."

With Mattie on one side and Liz on the other, they managed to coax the distraught woman back to her house. Liz saw Ezra coming out of the barn and called to him. "Ezra, could you go to the mercantile and tell my Uncle David we need him? If he's not there, Phillip will know where he is."

"Yes, Miss. I'll go straightaway."

Meg still did not speak. She let her maid guide her to a chair by the fireplace while Liz threw on more wood stoked the blaze.

"I'll make tea," Mattie offered, heading for the kitchen.

"We all need some to warm up," Liz agreed. She pulled a stool close to Meg and sat down. "Can you tell me what happened?"

Meg swallowed. Her lips moved, but no sound came.

"You tried to give Jamie some cookies," Liz prompted.

Meg nodded. "He saw me and ran for the creek," she croaked. She looked at Liz with pleading in her eyes. "I screamed for him to go back." Meg leaned her head back and closed her eyes.

"All the children have been taught that the currents make the ice unsafe near the bridge. You must remember when we were little how Grandpa George told us about it so often we would get angry with him."

Briefly Meg blinked her eyes. Liz felt sure her cousin heard and understood her. "This is not your fault." She took Meg's cold hands in her own. "Jamie might have run across there even if he had not seen you."

Meg shook her head from side to side. "It is my fault. He thought I beckoned to him, and he trusted me."

Liz looked up with a deep sigh. Just then Mattie came back with a tray. Gratefully, Liz accepted the tea and watched as Mattie put Meg's hands around a cup. "At least it will warm her hands," the maid said. "Has she spoken yet?"

Liz nodded her head. "She thinks the boy saw her beckon to him to cross."

Mattie's face wrinkled in disagreement. "No, no, Miss Margaret would never do anything like that. She has lived by this creek since she was a child herself. She knows the danger."

"I agree, but it is going to take awhile for Meg to accept that."

"What should we do?" Mattie questioned, looking out the window toward the people milling about by the creek.

Liz knew if the child had gone under the ice, there was no hope of saving him. "We need to take care of Meg. There are enough people out there. They don't need us."

A knock sounded at the door. Mattie jumped up from the edge of the chair she had perched on. "Mr. David wouldn't knock." She hurried to open the door.

"Pastor," Liz whispered in relief. "He will know what to do." She patted Meg on the knee as she rose to greet Pastor Ames.

He took Liz's hands. She could read the concern in his eyes. "Are you all right?"

Liz longed to fall against his chest and sob out her sorrow. Instead she murmured, "I'm fine. It is Meg who is still in shock."

He let go of her hands and went to greet Meg. The girl still sat with her head back and eyes closed, almost as if she were asleep. Only her lips moved. "I killed him, Pastor."

Shock registered on Pastor Ames's face. "What is she saying?" he asked Liz.

Liz came to his side and took Meg's teacup before her cousin dropped it. "She saw Jamie on the path and ran to meet him on the bridge with cookies. He must have seen her and tried to cut across the ice."

Pastor still looked confused. "Then what is she saying?"

"She believes the boy thought she beckoned to him to come across the creek."

Mattie came to the pastor with a cup of tea. "Please, will you sit down?" she invited.

He took the cup and sat on the chair opposite Meg. "Has she been like this ever since?"

"Yes," Liz nodded. "I was on my way home and heard a scream just as I started across the bridge. When I came back, Meg stood in the snow staring at the break in the ice. Mattie and I got her back here."

Pastor folded his hands and bowed his head. "I just heard about Jamie. I must get to Fannie and Tom." Looking up, he smiled at Liz. "But I had to make sure Meg was all right." His look softened. "And I am glad to see you are taking care of her."

Liz felt the heat on her face. "I will keep trying to comfort my cousin," she murmured. "Have you seen Aunt Sally?"

"No. I plan to stop and pick her up. She will want to be with her son and daughter-in-law." He stood, put his cup on the nearby table, and put his hands on Liz's shoulders. "Can you stay here for awhile? Meg shouldn't be alone."

Liz longed to step closer into his comforting embrace. She did not want to be the strong one, but she knew her duty. "I'll stay until Uncle David comes, but it's getting late, and my family will be worried."

"I won't leave Miss Margaret," Mattie declared. Liz turned to look at the woman who hovered nearby. Suddenly she realized the depth of Mattie's love for her cousin.

"I'll run home to feed my cat when Mr. David is here," Mattie explained, "but I'll stay with Miss Margaret until she is herself again."

"Thank you, Mattie. You are part of the family," Liz declared.

Meg reached up to take Mattie's hand. "Could you bring your cat here?" she asked in a voice that sounded like that of a child.

"You never wanted an animal in the house," Mattie said in surprise.

"I have been wrong many times," Meg whispered.

"I must go, Meg, but you are in good hands. I'll come back soon," Pastor Ames promised.

"You won't tell Tom and Fannie that I killed their son?"

Pastor Ames knelt beside Meg, brushing her hair back from her face. "You tried to save his life, not take it."

Meg's only response was to roll her head back and forth.

Pastor rose and smiled weakly at Mattie and Liz. "It will take us awhile to bring her around. Now I must go to the parents."

Liz walked him to the door. "Tell Aunt Sally I will bring Mother in as soon as I can."

Pastor Ames squeezed her hand. "I know Jamie was a favorite of yours. We will mourn him together." He added gently, "But I am going to need your help to get others through their grief."

❧

Uncle David returned home a few moments later. Walking directly to his daughter, he bent to kiss her cheek. "My poor baby. Are you going to be all right?"

Meg opened her eyes. Liz breathed a sigh of relief when she saw Meg's tears. It was the first sign that her cousin might be able to release some emotion. Meg's numb responses had scared Liz.

Uncle David stood to greet Mattie and Liz. "Thank you both for being here when she needed you." Smiling at Mattie, he continued, "You are always here for my daughter."

"She needs to feed the cat," Meg whispered.

Uncle David raised his eyebrows.

"I told her I would run home to feed the cat and come back to stay with her." Looking apologetic, she added, "Miss Margaret wanted me to bring the cat here."

"Whatever she wants." Uncle David patted Meg's head before turning to Liz. "It's dark out. Can you find your way home?"

"I must. My family will be frantic."

"Is your horse in my barn?"

"Yes. Ezra took care of her before he went to find you."

"I'll get lanterns for you and help you harness the mare."

"I'd appreciate a lantern, but I can harness the mare myself." She looked at her cousin. "Meg needs you with her."

❧

A short time later, Liz urged her mare back across the bridge. The snow reflected light from a full moon, so she felt sure she could follow the path home. The air was cold, and she wrapped the quilt tighter around her legs. Her faithful horse plodded on.

With her mind in a whirl, Liz let the animal find the way. She shuddered not from the cold but from the memories of the past few hours. *Jamie, precious Jamie. Everyone's favorite. So full of life. His bright copper curls a bright light on the darkest day. What will I tell the children?*

Liz let her thoughts turn to Scripture. *The answer is in the word of God,* she thought. *"The Lord is nigh unto them that are of a broken heart; and saveth such as be of a contrite spirit. Many are the afflictions of the righteous: but the Lord delivereth him out of them all."* The words of the psalm calmed her troubled spirit.

She let her mind play back Pastor Ames's words and the warmth in his look at her when he came to Meg's. *He said he would need my help. What can I possibly do? I'll pray for wisdom to comfort Jamie's friends and family.*

With her mind busy, the trip home did not seem to take long. She saw the lights from the house and barn and felt as if a great burden had been lifted.

Her father came out of the barn as Liz reined in the mare in the yard. He reached up without a word and pulled her off the sleigh into his arms. Liz felt like a little girl seeking comfort. She let her emotions go and sobbed into his coat as he held her.

"Are you all right?"

She nodded and sniffed. She looked past her father to see her brother coming from the barn. "I'll take care of the horse," Matthew called. "Is Liz hurt?"

"No," Father answered. "I'll take her inside. Then she can tell what has happened." Liz felt him take her hand and lead me back door.

Edie swept past their father to give her a big hug. Edie raced... ard in my life. Where have you been?" her. She had only p... of supper on the table. "If you'll bring ... ll you what has happened." stomach growled as her sister... sister's bidding. Liz watched vegetables. Liz hung up her cloak... something to do, but her ... the thick broth and who still sat at the table. ... kiss her mother,

"It is sad news," Liz warned them. Then she told the family what had transpired that afternoon. "I'm so sorry I am late, but I couldn't leave Meg in the state she was in. Pastor Ames came for a few minutes, but he wanted to go to Aunt Sally and to Jamie's parents."

Tears filled her mother's eyes.

Liz quickly said, "I told Pastor to tell Aunt Sally you would come as soon as you could."

Mama nodded. "You are a good girl, my daughter."

Liz ate the soup and it warmed her body, but it seemed nothing would drive out the chill that had settled on her heart since she'd realized Jamie was gone.

eight

As Liz ate her soup, E[illegible] the table. With the dishes out of the way, th[illegible] girl placed the family Bible in front of their fa[illegible]ing hands, the family prayed for Jamie and his famil[illegible]

Liz w[illegible] her father page through the Bible. "Please read Psal[illegible]34, Father."

He looked up with a smile. "That's what I turned to."

"I kept repeating the words of the last verses as I drove the sleigh home." She sighed. "It brought comfort."

They all listened as Father read God's promises to deliver them from the afflictions of a broken heart.

Liz watched her sister, who looked puzzled. Edie looked at their mother and asked, "Why didn't Jamie crawl out of the hole he fell in?"

Liz reached to take the girl's hand.

"We have told you how the currents are swift by the bridge," their father said. "That means the water is deep and it moves fast. When Jamie fell in, his body was pulled under the ice by the current. He wouldn't have been able to find the hole again." His voice was heavy with sorrow.

"How will they find him?" Edie asked, still gripping Liz's hand.

Father sighed. "I don't know, Sweetheart. The men can't go out on the ice for fear of falling through. It may be spring before the child's body is found."

"Oh," Edie said, the horror apparent on her face. "Will he still go to heaven?"

Liz listened with rapt attention. She might need her father's wisdom to answer these same questions tomorrow in her schoolroom.

Father smiled softly. "We won't need our bodies in heaven. Jamie's soul is already with the Lord."

"You mean when I die and go to heaven, I get a new body without scars?"

"That's what Jesus promised us. There will be no more pain or suffering."

Liz squeezed her sister's hand. "Just don't be in a hurry to leave us, Edie. We need you and love you right with us."

"I will go to heaven someday, won't I?" Edie asked.

In answer, Father thumbed through his well-worn Bible to John 11 and read, " 'Jesus said unto her, I am the resurrection, and the life: he that believeth in me, though he were dead, yet shall he live. And whosoever liveth and believeth in me shall never die. Believest thou this?' "

"Oh, yes, Papa, I believe in Jesus as my Lord and Savior."

Mama wiped away a tear, then said, "It grows late, Jonathan. The children need to get to bed."

Father closed the Bible and laid it on the table. He took Emily's hand as the family again bowed their heads in prayer for the many who mourned for Jamie.

❧

The next morning, Liz and Edie were in the kitchen stirring up the fire and starting breakfast when their father came in from doing chores in the barn. "Looks like a storm brewing," he told them as he took the proffered cup of coffee.

"I must get to school."

"You can get to town, but watch the weather. You may have to start back early if the snow falls too hard. You won't be able to see the road."

"I'll be careful. What about Mother? She is going to want to go to Aunt Sally."

"I'll bundle her into the wagon. I have the runners on it and can get her to town for a short visit."

Liz glanced at her sister, who was breaking eggs into a pan on the stove.

"I'll need you to go with me to help take care of your mother, Edie." Father smiled in answer to Liz's unanswered question. "We won't stay long. As soon as it starts to snow, I will insist your mother come home. Sally will understand."

"I'm sure she will. I'll go in early this morning to let her know your plans." Liz took a sip of coffee. "I don't know what do to about Meg. I should spend some time with her."

"You come home, Child. David will take responsibility for his daughter," Father said firmly.

"Yes, Papa. I know Pastor will spend time with Meg. I just hope the storm doesn't last a long time. I'd like to go back to comfort her." She put the cup down and took the piece of bread Edie offered her. "She really believes she is responsible for Jamie running onto the ice."

"She would never do that," Edie said, putting a plate of eggs in front of Father.

"No, she wouldn't, but right now she's feeling guilty."

"Aw, she's just looking for attention," Matthew said, joining the family at the table.

"You're wrong, Matthew," Liz said, getting up. "This is different. Meg is grieving, and I want to comfort her. Now I better help Mother get dressed. I need to start for school."

❧

The clouds hung low and threatening as dawn broke over the countryside. Liz coaxed the mare to a faster pace.

Reaching Aunt Sally's home, she quickly settled the mare for the day and hurried into the kitchen. Liz stopped and tried to mask the shock she felt at her aunt's appearance. The woman looked ten years older than when Liz had last seen her. Liz pressed her cheek against her aunt's gray, wrinkled face.

"I must get to school, but I had to see you first. Are you all right?"

"As well as can be expected. I certainly never wanted to outlive my grandchildren." Aunt Sally turned away. "He will never grow up." Her voice wavered. "God called another child to His heavenly garden."

"You will always have the image of his bright, strawberry-colored hair and wide grin in your heart," Liz whispered gently.

Surprised, Aunt Sally turned to face Liz. "You are right, Elizabeth. Not only will I always have a small grandson in my heart, he will be waiting for me in heaven."

"How is Fannie?"

"Still in shock. She and Tom are both devastated. Pastor stayed with them until late last night."

"Mother will be here soon. Father said he would bring her and Edie to visit for a short time. He thinks we are in for a storm and won't let Mother stay after it starts to snow."

Aunt Sally smiled weakly. "It's good of her to come out when I know the price she pays in pain."

"It would be more painful for her not to be with you." Liz patted Aunt Sally's hand. "Now I must be on my way to school. The children will have questions, and I want to be there for them."

"Pastor is there now. He said he would stay with you to help calm the youngsters."

At the sound of his name, Liz felt a warm glow fill her being. "He is so thoughtful," she murmured.

"He told me how good you were with Meg yesterday. I know he felt badly to have to leave you with her, but he was right to go to Fannie and Tom."

"Father made me promise to come home early today, so I won't be able to visit Meg. But I'll go back as soon as the weather permits."

Aunt Sally reached out to hug Liz. "God bless you, Child. You are so like your mother. Always thinking of others."

Liz hurried to the school. She saw the smoke rising from the chimney and thanked God for Pastor Ames, who always had a fire going in the stove before she got there. Opening the door, she saw him seated at a desk near the stove, reading. Liz paused to drink in the sight of him.

Pastor Ames turned to smile at her. "Come sit where it is warm," he invited, motioning to the crackling fire in the stove.

"I stopped to visit with Aunt Sally. She looks so haggard and worn, she tore at my heart."

"She'll need extra love to get through her grief, Liz. We will be there to help her survive this tragedy."

"What about Fannie and Tom?"

"They will never be the same. Losing a child, especially like this, will leave scars forever." He sighed and closed his Bible. "They may even have questions about why God would let it happen."

"But God didn't make Jamie run onto the ice," Liz protested.

Pastor looked at her and nodded. "You are correct, but it will take the boy's parents awhile to recognize that the Lord cries with them." He stood next to Liz. "Would you like me to help you with your students today?"

Liz nodded. "I'd appreciate having you here."

Slowly the children filed into school and took their seats. They were quiet, and Liz missed the usual banter that took place between her students. As each one came in, Liz greeted them warmly and tried to dispel some of the gloom. As soon as the desks were filled, she spoke. "I am sure you have all heard that Jamie Davis fell through the ice and died yesterday. Pastor Ames is here with us today. I would like him to lead us in prayer for our missing classmate."

Liz heard a sniff or two from some of the older girls. Pastor stepped forward. "Let's bow our heads in prayer." His voice spread over the students. "Dear Lord, we remember before Thee our friend and Thy faithful servant, Jamie Davis. We know Thou has opened to him the gates of a larger life, and we pray Thou wilt receive him more and more into Thy joyful service. We pray that we may faithfully serve Thee until we too share in the eternal victory of Jesus Christ our Lord. Amen." The children repeated his "amen" with what Liz thought was surprising strength.

"Thank you, Pastor," Liz said, stepping to his side. "Pastor Ames has said we are to remember our friend, and I invite you to tell us what Jamie meant in your life." Looking around, she saw William wavering on the edge of tears. The boy bravely put his hand in the air. Liz nodded to him.

"Jamie walked home from school with me." William looked down and Liz could see tears drip on the desktop. "We crossed the creek up near my house where it is safe to skate." William looked up and wiped his wet cheeks with the back of his hand. "I don't know why Jamie walked back the other way. I'm sorry he crossed the creek on the ice and didn't go on the bridge."

"We will never know why he did that, William, but it does teach us to listen and obey the rules whether they be from God or from our parents."

One by one the children spoke of Jamie. As time wore on, some of the stories became a reflection of the bright, joyful boy Jamie had been. Standing side-by-side, Pastor Ames and Liz encouraged the children to remember Jamie and the good times they had shared.

Liz kept glancing out the window. She saw the snow start to fall. By midmorning the wind had picked up, and the falling flakes swirled in the yard.

"We are in for a storm, so I'm going to close school early today. We want all of you to get home safely. You know we will not have school if your parents say it is not safe for you to be out."

As the children started to gather their belongings out of their desks, Liz suggested, "Let's ask Pastor to send us off with a blessing."

His voice rang out with the words, "Go in peace to love and serve the Lord."

Pastor Ames and Liz helped the children into their coats and scarves and sent them on their way.

"You're good with children, Liz. Letting them talk about Jamie made his death seem less frightening to them."

Liz sighed and looked up at him. Seeing his admiration made her cheeks burn. "It helped to have you here with us."

"I hope to always be there when you need me," he said, touching her cheek.

It would be so easy to rest my head on his shoulder. To let him comfort me would be wonderful, Liz thought. She stepped back as another thought crowded out her dream.

"I promised my father I would come home when the snow started. I won't be able to stop and see Meg today."

The pastor sighed deeply and let his hand fall from her cheek. "I'll stop by there this afternoon. I know you will visit her when you can." He smiled tenderly. "I will give her your regards. Now let's get you back to your sleigh and on your way home." He took her cloak and wrapped it around her. She felt his hands linger a moment on her shoulders and shivered in delight.

nineteen

The storm raged for three days. The wind swirled great drifts of snow against the Millers' barn. Each morning Matthew and his father would dig a path to get to their animals.

"You don't have to worry about an open winter slowing the syrup harvest," Mama teased Father when he came in shivering from the cold one afternoon.

"Let me pour you hot coffee, Papa," Edie offered, entering from the parlor.

"How is the quilting coming?" Jonathan asked, taking the cup his daughter offered.

"We have one tied and have started on a second," Liz said, joining the family in the kitchen. "Mother has been busy sewing quilt tops since last fall."

Liz saw the smile her mother gave her father. "We may need to furnish another house," Mama said with a twinkle in her eye.

"Not for me," Matthew protested. "Jane's father says she has to be eighteen before she can marry."

Liz looked from one parent to the other and wished she could read their minds. They seemed to be able to communicate without words. *Must be from living together for so long,* she thought.

"What have you got to eat? I'm hungry," Matthew said, hanging up his coat.

"I have stew simmering on the back of the stove, but it's for supper. Would you like some leftover corn bread?" Edie offered.

"That would be fine." Matthew started to pour a cup of coffee. "I hear a horse. Who would be out in this weather?" He put his cup on the table and went to the window. "It's Pastor." Matthew grabbed his coat and went out the door.

Liz saw the look of pleasure on Edie's face. The girl turned to her mother. "Could I stop quilting and bake a pie?"

"Don't you think we should wait to see if the pastor plans to stay?"

"Matthew will eat it," Edie coaxed.

Liz smiled. "Do you want me to peel apples?"

"Yes, please," Edie said, taking down a mixing bowl.

By the time the men entered the kitchen, the girls were busy cooking.

"What brings you out?" Father asked. "Not more bad news, I hope."

Pastor went to warm his hands over the stove. "No. The weather has brought things to a standstill." His look lingered on Liz, making her cheeks grow hot. "I've checked on the schoolhouse but won't bother with a fire till the weather breaks," he told her.

"How is Sally?" Mama asked.

Pastor Ames took the cup of coffee Matthew poured. "She mourns for the boy, but her faith keeps her strong. She's a great help to Fannie." He took a sip of coffee and sat at the table with Father. "Fannie is angry with the world right now. She wants to lash out at God, but in her heart she knows the Lord didn't cause the accident that took Jamie."

"And Meg?" Liz asked quietly.

Pastor sighed and put his cup down. "She broods. She still blames herself." He looked thoughtful. "I think she feels guilty for more than Jamie's death."

"She has a lot to feel guilty for," Matthew growled.

"That's not for us to say, Matthew," Father cautioned. "You know how we're told in Romans 2 not to judge others."

Silence filled the room. Liz stood with the coffeepot in her hand and watched Matthew. He looked at the floor. She thought she heard him mutter, "I'm sorry."

"Meg is beginning to regret some of her past," Pastor interjected, breaking the silence. "It's up to us to teach her of the

Lord's forgiveness." He held his cup for Liz to refill. "That's one reason I came out today."

He turned to Father. "I'd like to ask Liz to help me with Meg."

"Fine with me," Father said with a shrug. "What do you think she can do?"

"She and Edie started with the Christmas pageant. Meg found out she liked to do things for people. This tragedy with Jamie has set her back. I think she will come around, but I need Liz to talk woman to woman with her."

"Me?" Liz turned from the stove, where she had put the coffeepot to keep it warm. "What can I do?"

"If your father will trust me to take you to town in this bad weather, I'd like you to come with me and talk to Meg. Together we can teach her Scriptures that explain forgiveness."

"We can't go now," she protested, looking out the window at the darkening landscape.

"I could come early in the morning and take your sleigh to town." He turned to Father. "The Evanses have cleared the drifts by their place."

"If I can get to town, I should open the school," Liz protested.

"None of the parents will be sending their children out in this weather. By the time the drifts from this storm have been cleared, another one will move in," Father predicted. "Be awhile before school starts again."

Liz looked to her mother in confusion.

"I think it would be a good idea for Liz to help you," Mama said to the pastor, not missing a stitch on the socks she knitted. "It'd be a good experience for her."

Smells of baking apple pies filled the room. Edie looked in the oven and then turned to Pastor. "Will you stay for supper?"

"Hard to turn down that offer, but I need to find my way back to town before dark."

"Stay the night," Matthew offered. He had sat quietly while the men talked. "I'll share my room, and it'll save you coming back for my sister in the morning."

"Does Sally know you came out here?" Father asked.

Pastor Ames nodded his head.

"Good, then it's set. She'll know where you are." He turned to Edie. "How about some of your biscuits to go with that stew you promised?"

Liz basked in the camaraderie her family and the pastor shared as the evening continued. She sat quietly at the kitchen table with the others, listening to her father and the pastor make plans to complete the church.

"Once the church is built, I plan to put up a small house at the foot of the orchard by the road," Father announced. Liz looked up from her cup in surprise.

"Got a nice spring nearby for water," he added.

"A pretty view," Mama commented.

Liz looked from one parent to the other. When had they decided to do this?

"You looking for a tenant?" Pastor asked with a smile.

"Have one in mind," Father said, holding his cup toward Liz for a refill.

Liz stood to fetch the coffeepot. Her mind whirled.

After filling the cups, she sat back down but did not listen to the rest of the conversation. Could her parents possibly think she would marry and live down the road? Watching Pastor Ames, Liz dreamed that such a thing could happen.

❧

The morning dawned clear and bright. The two girls were up early to prepare breakfast for the family, and Liz and Pastor were on the road soon after the sun came up.

"Meg will not be up this early," Liz protested, as she pulled the quilt closer around her legs in the sleigh, trying to keep warm.

"We'll go visit your aunt Sally first. I need to check on her after leaving her alone last night."

"Is she really going to be all right? She looked so haggard when I saw her last."

"Jamie's death has been hard on her. A death out of season is the most difficult to accept. No one wants to lose a child."

"I can't think what it would be like. We almost lost Edie, and that seemed an endless nightmare." Liz looked at the sparkling snow without seeing it. "There were times when she cried so in pain, I prayed the Lord would take her."

"Times like that, you are prepared a little for death, but when it comes through an accident, no one knows how to respond. Fannie's feelings of anger are not unusual. We will just have to stay close to them and pray for all of the family."

Liz looked at the man beside her. He said "we," but what did he mean by that? Was he speaking of the entire congregation or of just the two of them?

❧

Stephen glanced over at Liz. His heart soared to be so close to her in this winter wonderland. He shifted the reins to one hand and took her gloved hand in his. "Are you warm enough?"

She smiled up at him and nodded.

"You are so kind and thoughtful toward everyone. I appreciate your coming with me to visit Meg."

"I'm not sure what good I will be."

"You will be at my side, and together we will help her." He slipped his hand free from his glove and touched her cheek. "I would like to have you at my side for the rest of my life."

She looked down, but not before he saw the glow on her face.

Looking back at the road, he pulled the horse to a stop. "I spoke to your father, and he has given me permission to ask you to marry me," he said quietly. Turning back to her with a smile, he continued, "Your father said he and your mother would welcome me into your family."

Stephen gently placed his finger under her chin, caressing the side of her jaw with his thumb. She looked up at him with amber eyes that reflected both hope and hesitation.

"I love you, Liz," Stephen said. "I've been drawn to you from the first moment I saw on you in church that first Sunday I was here. You have taught me so much about patience and servanthood."

"Me?" Liz questioned. "I've taught you? But you're the pastor," she protested.

"Yes, and like all pastors, I'm quite human with much to learn. Your life is an example of faith in action, and I can think of nothing that would make me happier than to hear that you love me too and will marry me." He paused and gave a smile full of mischief. "Maybe I could even convince you to call me 'Stephen' when we are in private and you don't have to worry about scandalizing the church folks by calling your pastor by his first name."

A becoming blush stained Liz's cheeks. "I do love you, Stephen," she admitted, "although I've tried so hard not to. I didn't see how I could marry you and still be able to help my family. And I worried that Meg would be upset, and that if you chose me as your wife, her condition would become even worse."

"But don't you see, Dear," Stephen countered, "I love your family too. You don't have to choose between us. We will both help them whenever they need our support. And as for Meg, we aren't responsible for her choices. God only asks us to walk in His ways, to show her His love, and to leave the results with Him."

Stephen watched her beloved face carefully to see if his words had helped answer her questions. Then he knew. Love shone from her eyes, and joy radiated from her face.

"Will you marry me?" he asked.

"Oh, yes!" Liz exclaimed.

He lowered his lips to hers and drew her into his arms. The moment he had dreamed of for so long had finally come true, and Stephen knew his greatest imaginings could not compare to the reality of holding the woman he loved and hearing her promise to be with him for the rest of their lives.

❧

When the couple entered Aunt Sally's kitchen, the old lady looked at them and smiled. "You bring joy into my house," she said, enveloping Liz in a warm hug.

"How did you know?" Liz asked.

"Oh, you do not have to say a word, Child. The glow on your faces says it all. I am so pleased for you both."

Insisting that they sit in the parlor and let her serve tea, Aunt Sally set about getting down cups and the tea caddy. Liz followed Stephen and sat next to him on the settee. He took her hands, now free of mittens, and she felt her heart expand in joy.

"I am glad you chose to tell Aunt Sally first," she told him. "She needed to have something to ease the sorrow of losing Jamie."

He smiled at her. "We all need something joyful to look forward to. You have no idea how much I have dreamed of this day."

Aunt Sally came in with a tray of cookies and tea. As she served them, she asked, "What are your plans?"

Liz felt the blush spread over her face. "I have no plans, but from what I have heard my parents saying, they have lots of ideas for us." The sparkle in Aunt Sally's eyes gave Liz a warm feeling. "Have you and my mother been talking?"

Aunt Sally's laugh betrayed her. "We have been hoping this would happen. Will you tell the congregation soon?" she asked Stephen.

He sighed and squeezed Liz's hand. "Because of Meg's condition right now, we will talk to her before we announce our wedding plans to the congregation."

"That is why Father let me come to town today," Liz added. "Pastor asked me to go with him to talk to Meg." She looked at him and smiled. "I thought we were going to teach her about the Lord's forgiveness."

His look made her tingle. "We will do that also," he said.

Aunt Sally put her teacup down. "You know her grandmother was not stable. The woman became bedridden and dependent on laudanum."

Stephen looked surprised. "I didn't know that, but we will make sure it does not happen to Meg."

❧

After enjoying the tea with Aunt Sally, the young couple went to call on Meg. Mattie met them at the door and invited them to come in by the fireplace in the parlor.

Liz went to her cousin's side and knelt next to her chair. She had never seen Meg look disheveled before. The girl sat with her hair brushed loose around her shoulders. She wore a dressing gown and sat with Mattie's cat curled up in her lap. "How are you, Meg?" Liz asked.

Meg looked at her and then at Stephen. "You came out in the storm?"

"Pastor came out to the farm and brought me in to see you. I have been worried about you." Liz took Meg's hand. "Did you take a chill from being out in the snow without a cloak?"

Meg shook her head. "I have been sitting here trying to count all my sins."

Liz looked at Stephen, appalled. He must have seen her concern because he knelt on the other side of Meg. "Meg," he said, "remember God's promise in the Bible: 'For I will be merciful to their unrighteousness, and their sins and their iniquities will I remember no more.' " His voice held firm conviction.

Meg appeared not to have heard him. She looked at Liz with a blank stare. "I have said bad things about your sister."

"You are Edie's friend. She doesn't remember anything but your helping bake cookies for Christmas." Liz patted her cousin's hand. "You made her feel so proud when you asked her to make hot chocolate after skating." She watched Meg's face for a hint of emotion.

Turning to Stephen, Meg asked, "How could God punish my sins by taking a child's life?"

"God did not do that, Meg. You called out to Jamie trying to save his life. You are not to blame for him running out on the unsafe ice."

"But people will think I am. I always do bad things," she muttered, stroking the cat.

Liz looked at Stephen and sighed.

Mattie came into the room with cups of tea and urged them to sit down in the chairs near the fire. "Will you drink some tea?" the woman asked Meg. The girl shook her head apathetically.

Serving Liz and Stephen, Mattie explained, "She isn't eating much."

"Are you staying here?" Stephen asked, accepting the tea.

"Yes," Mattie said as she tried to coax Meg to take a cup. "Mr. David helped me close up my place and bring my things here." She patted Meg's hair. "She seems to like my cat," she said and smiled. "And there's no doubt old KitKat loves the attention."

The young couple spent more time trying to talk to Meg. When they left, Liz asked Stephen, "Do you think we did any good?"

"She will come out of it. I'm sure of it. But it will take time and lots of prayer." He took Liz's hand. "I trust the Lord to show us how to help her." He looked out over the snow and added, "Acts twenty-six, verse eighteen tells us, 'To open their eyes, and to turn them from darkness to light, and from the power of Satan unto God, that they may receive forgiveness of sins.' " He smiled at Liz. "That is our task."

Liz watched Stephen's profile and vowed silently to be a good wife. She snuggled close to his side as they traveled back to her home to share their joy with her family.

twenty

Father's prediction of one storm after another proved to be correct. Through most of February, the roads remained impassable. The fresh snow was difficult for the horses to navigate, and the sleigh sank into the drifts.

"How can I teach the children if they cannot get to school?" Liz worried, looking out of the kitchen window at still more falling snow.

"Spring will come, and you will have them back in class," her mother said in encouragement. "We had a winter like this the first year we lived here. The snow piled to the roof of the cabin. My sister and I thought we would never get out again." Mama chuckled. "I chafed at being housebound, but sweet Beth remained cheerful."

Liz's mother smiled. "Meg is like her mother. She's not as selfish or mean as some believed."

Liz sat on the stool at her mother's feet. "Stephen and I talk to her about forgiveness. I wonder if she even hears us?"

"She does. It will take awhile for her to accept your words. Something will happen that will bring her out of the state she has fallen into. And remember, you not only use your own words, you quote the Word of God. He will use His words to bring healing to her soul."

Liz sighed. "Sometimes it's a struggle to trust God, but you're right. We must place Meg in God's hands."

"Does Meg know you and Stephen plan to marry?"

Shaking her head, Liz said, "No. We want her to be more stable before we tell her." She smiled at her mother. "Stephen says that regardless of how Meg responds, we will be married."

"Good. I never understood why you thought you had to stand aside for her in the first place."

Liz looked down at her folded hands that rested in her lap. "I felt sorry for her. She always seemed to make trouble for herself."

"Compassion is good, Liz. Just remember you cannot save Meg by yourself. Trust the Lord. He has a plan for your cousin."

❧

Matthew and the Evans boys worked to keep the road to town open. They stuck long sticks upright in the snow to mark the way, and between storms, they snowshoed along the path to pack the snow down. "Look who I found wandering in the snow," Matthew called one afternoon as he entered the kitchen from outdoors.

Liz jumped up to greet Stephen. "You walked out here in the snow?"

"Take more than snow to keep me away. Where is my favorite cook?" He looked around the kitchen.

"Edie is in the root cellar sorting apples," Mama explained from her rocker. "Any that have started to go bad are fed to the deer. The winter snows make it hard for them to find feed."

"The deer have kept us in winter meat for years, so we are just taking care of them like we do the cows and pigs," Matthew said, hanging up his coat.

"Are you here to take Liz into town?" Mama asked in a worried tone. "The weather doesn't look good."

"No. I came to see the family. The weather is so bad, I find it difficult to get around to visit everyone in the congregation. We haven't had more than a handful in church for the last two weeks."

"We haven't held school in two weeks," Liz noted. "The children will have forgotten everything they learned this year. I'm copying down arithmetic problems for them to take home and work on when we can open school again. I wish they had books to read," she lamented.

"They have the Bible. Give them verses to memorize," Stephen suggested. "Or you could assign them books from the Old Testament. The boys could write stories about men like Joseph, Daniel, or David, and the girls could write about Rebecca, Ruth, or Esther. Then they will be both reading and writing."

"You have a wonderful idea," Liz enthused. "Then we can read the stories when school starts again." She walked to his side. "Will you help me pick out the verses? I'll have the little ones memorize verses and the older children write stories."

❧

Gradually the storms came farther apart. After three weeks, Liz was able to teach again. The children welcomed the tasks she assigned for the days they could not come to school. "Sure beats shoveling snow," one of the older boys said when he stood to read his story about David.

Liz made it a point to close school early enough so she could visit Meg at least once a week. Her cousin had started to take an interest in her appearance again. Finally the afternoon came when Meg wore a pretty bodice and skirt. Her hair was put up as Meg always used to wear it.

Noting Meg's changed appearance, Liz said, "You look very nice, Meg. Are you feeling better?"

Meg got up to greet Liz with a hug, "You are kind to keep coming to see me. Aunt Sally and Aunt Fannie were here earlier." She urged her cousin to sit down. "I want to read you something." She picked up her Bible. "Pastor says you are giving the children verses to memorize, and he assigned one to me." She smiled as she opened the book. "It is Ephesians, the fourth chapter, and the thirty-second verse: 'And be ye kind one to another, tender-hearted, forgiving one another, even as God for Christ's sake hath forgiven you.' "

Meg looked up with a smile. "This verse describes you."

Embarrassed, Liz stuttered, "What Pastor means is that by the grace of God we are forgiven."

Meg giggled. "I think what the pastor is saying is that I should be more like you."

The conversation was not going in the direction Liz would have chosen. "Meg, I'm confused."

"Oh, Liz, when will you stop being so blind?"

"Me, blind!" Liz exclaimed.

"Pastor Ames loves you. Why don't you see that?" Meg asked with a smile.

"Would you mind if that were true?" Liz asked timidly.

Meg's laugh echoed in the room. "But he does love you, Liz. Why do you try to hide it? I'm not going to try to sabotage your relationship with him. I've changed."

Liz watched her cousin, wondering what had happened to the girl. This was not the Meg she knew.

Meg walked over and knelt by Liz. "I've spent a lot of time thinking this winter. You and Pastor have come often and given me food for thought." She covered her cousin's hands with her own. "I have come to know the Lord. I will trust Him to guide me, and I will stop trying to manipulate the world to make it conform to what I want."

Tears ran down Liz's face. She reached out to hug Meg. "Lots of people have prayed for you to come to this place." She slipped to her knees beside her cousin. "Let's pray together. Lord, forgive us for the times we have hurt people. Give us faith to believe that Thou hast forgiven us."

As the girls prayed and hugged, KitKat came to rub against Meg. His purring turned their tears to laughter.

"It sounds good to hear laughter in this house," Mattie said, coming into the parlor. "What is the occasion?"

"We are going to plan Liz's wedding," Meg said, pulling Liz to her feet.

❧

Spring arrived at last. Mud filled the roads, so Liz rode the mare and left the buggy at home. "Only until the roads dry up," she promised her mother, who frowned on ladies riding horseback into town.

"How will you be able to bring home that cream-colored lace I had David order?" Mama protested.

"Mother, I won't be married until summer. You don't need that lace right now." Liz hung up her cloak. "Are Father and Matthew back from making maple syrup yet?"

"Your father came in today to bring boxes of sugar. He says the sap is still running. It may be two more weeks before they stop tapping the trees and close up camp."

"He took all the food I had cooked and baked for them," Edie said. She smiled shyly. "He said Ezra and Clyde like my cooking."

"I'm glad they have help this year. With all the extra trees they've tapped, it takes four of them to boil down the syrup," Mama noted as she continued knitting at a good pace.

"I thought Stephen would help them," Liz said thoughtfully.

"He's busy getting things lined up to finish building the church." Her mother smiled. "I think he wants a proper church to be married in."

"I stopped to see Meg today."

"Is she still cheerful?" Edie asked.

"She and Mattie have the house torn up cleaning. The new doctor is due in town, and Uncle David invited him to stay there until he can find a place of his own."

"How is Mattie with the new arrangement?" Mama inquired.

Liz shrugged her shoulders. "She seems fine. She told me today her sister's boy is coming out from Connecticut and she will give him her house." She looked at her mother, puzzled. "I don't understand why Mattie has stayed in her own house all these years."

"Maybe she felt more independent with a place of her own," Edie said.

Liz hugged her sister around the waist. "You could be right. But Meg and Mattie seem to get along fine now."

Turning back to her mother, she added, "Mattie said her nephew is bringing his new bride. Maybe she would be willing to help out here sometimes. When I move out, Edie may need more help in the house."

"I don't like to think about you living somewhere else," Edie pouted.

"I'll only be down the road," Liz said, laughing, "and I'll probably have to come get cooking lessons from you."

❧

Stephen had pulled the canvas off the stacks of wood as soon the weather cleared. He sorted through them to make sure th boards were still sound. Men in his congregation who had experience building came to help him decide how much more lumber they would need.

"Going to be a big building, Pastor."

"I plan to fill it," Stephen said with confidence.

"Hear you plan on marrying the schoolmistress," his companion said.

"Yes. I hope to have this built so we can be married here in the summer," Stephen told the men.

"Be sorry to lose her as a teacher. My boys would never have stayed in school this long if it hadn't been for her." He shrugged. "I don't know if they'll go to the new school or not. Guess we'll have to wait and see how much it'll cost to send them there."

"Is that building about finished?" Stephen asked.

"They did a lot of finishing work on the inside this winter. Thanks to your helping get the mortar to harden when the weather got cold, they got the roof on and started on the inside before snow came."

"Good. I know Mr. Howard wants the school to open this year. He's offered to let us use the building, but I hope we will have our own church by then."

"I'll give all the time I can, Pastor, but you know the crops have to go in the ground as soon as the earth warms up."

"With many of us working, it will go up fast," Stephen said confidently, looking at the sky as if seeing the building silhouetted against the fluffy clouds that drifted by. Pulling himself back to the present, he wrote down what his helpers suggested he get for building supplies. "I'll talk to David Miller and see what we can do about getting these things," he told the men.

A few minutes later, they parted company, and Stephen rode to the mercantile.

"My father went home, Pastor," Phillip said. "The new doctor ne today, and he is going to stay at our house for awhile. Father took him to get settled in."

After a brief visit with Phillip, Stephen decided to go by the Miller house. Leaving his horse tethered in the yard, he strode to the front door.

"Oh, come in, Pastor," invited a breathless Meg. "Liz is in the parlor." She closed the door behind him and hurriedly ushered him forward.

Stephen stopped in the doorway when he saw Liz standing next to a handsome man. Jealousy reared its ugly head. This stranger stood at least six feet tall. His ginger-colored hair and mustache gave him a dashing look. The man was clad in a good black suit with a white shirt and tie. Stephen looked down at his dirty boots, old work pants, and homespun shirt. Again, he looked at Liz standing in her neat black skirt and pretty print bodice. *Why would she bother with me?* he wondered.

Liz looked up, and when she saw Stephen, his doubts vanished. He could feel the love she radiated toward him. He looked down as Meg pulled at his sleeve.

"Come meet Dr. Brewster, Pastor." She urged him toward the stranger, who held out his hand.

"Miss Elizabeth has been telling me about you," the doctor said.

Liz smiled at Stephen and then at Meg. Stephen followed her gaze and saw the glow on Meg's face.

So that is how it is to be, he thought with an inward smile. Looking back at Liz, he gave a faint nod. He didn't think much time would pass before a second wedding would be in the works.

twenty-one

"Do you have a list of things you need from the mercantile?" Liz asked her mother a couple weeks later. "Father thinks the road to town has dried up enough so I can take the buggy today."

"Edwina put my list on the shelf by the cups. I hope that lace is here," Mama fretted.

Liz bent to kiss her mother's cheek. "You have made me a beautiful dress even if you did not put lace around the inset in the bodice. Will you start on Edie's dress now?"

Mama smiled. "Have you talked her into standing up with you?"

"Stephen will talk her into it even if she won't listen to us." Liz chuckled. "May I look for some pretty print for her dress?"

Her mother nodded. "She'll think she should wear homespun, but I think a pretty dress will please her."

Liz worked hard with her students that day, continuing to help them catch up for all the time they had missed because of snow. The hours passed quickly. After school, when she stopped by to get her horse and buggy, Liz knocked on Aunt Sally's back door. Hearing no answer, she figured Aunt Sally was visiting her daughter-in-law, who was still distraught after the death of her son Jamie.

Liz stopped in front of the mercantile and fastened the mare's reins to a post. "Hello, Phillip. How are you?" she said to her cousin as she stepped inside.

"I thought you were still snowed in. Haven't seen you for weeks," he complained.

"I've been riding horseback and couldn't carry packages. Now the road is dry enough for the buggy. Mother has a list of things she needs. Did the lace come in?"

"Yes. I'll get it for you."

...he disappeared into the back room, Liz started looking ...ough the bolts of cloth. Her dress material had a cream back-...ound with pink flowers. She took out a piece with a similar ...background and blue flowers. "Maybe there will be enough of the lace to trim Edie's dress too," she murmured.

"You talking to me?" Phillip asked.

Liz giggled. "No, I'm talking to myself." She carried the bolt of cloth to the counter. "How is Meg? I haven't been to see her yet this week."

"She is a pleasure to be around. The Lord certainly worked miracles in her," he said with a note of wonder. "And now with the doctor here, she is even more fun to be around."

"Is Dr. Brewster still staying with you?"

Phillip grinned. "No, he took rooms at the hotel. He said it was not proper for him to court Meg while he lived at our house."

"Court Meg." Liz dropped the bolt of cloth with a bang.

Phillip nodded with a pleased smile. "He asked Father for permission, and my sister is all smiles. She simply glows. Maybe you can have a double wedding."

Stunned, Liz said, "I could see she was smitten, but I did not know the doctor felt the same way. What does Uncle David think of all this?"

"He is so busy with the town commission, I'm not sure he has given it much thought."

"We missed having him help with the syrup this year."

"I am sure he would have liked to help out. I must admit I miss having him here as often as usual too."

"What's keeping the commission so busy? They have the doctor they wanted," Liz said.

"The town is growing, and they are busy plotting out building lots and new streets for Millersville. My father bought the lot across the street from here."

"Whatever for?"

Phillip smiled. "He plans to build a brick building for our mercantile."

"I hadn't heard that. I wonder if my father knows."

"He must. He and my father met yesterday with the p planning how to get supplies for the new church."

"So much is happening."

"You should get your head out of the clouds and come visi me more often," he teased. "I hear your father is building another house."

Liz felt the blush. "Yes, he kept Clyde and Ezra on after the sap run and has them clearing an area by the orchard."

"So you will be able to stay close to home."

"Yes." She nodded her head. "Neither Stephen nor I want to be far from Edie."

"Will she live with you?"

Liz shook her head. "No, Mother needs her." She looked up in interest at Phillip. "Would you know of a woman in the village who could help out sometimes? We need someone to come a few days a week to help Edie. It's too much for her to do alone, especially now that she is cooking for the hired men too."

"You need to talk to Meg. She goes over to the Jenkins place a lot. Maybe one of their girls could use the work."

"I didn't know Meg did that."

Phillip grinned. "You started it when you suggested she give the littlest Jenkins child the shawl she knit." He leaned his hands on the counter. "My sister has learned to be more like you."

"She has learned she likes doing for others, just as the Bible tells us we should," Liz said.

"She'll be able to take the poor in if she wants. Dr. Brewster has bought an acre lot on what will be Jefferson Street. Says he is putting up a huge house that will hold his offices too."

"You are full of news, Phillip. I am going to bring mother in just so she can visit with you. Better yet, why don't you come out for supper? I'll even ask Edie to bake you a mincemeat pie."

"No fair. You know that's my favorite. What night do you want me?"

"Do you work late on Wednesdays?"

…, that will be perfect. I look forward to it."

…ow I better get these things Mother wants and start home."

❧

…arrying parcels into the house a bit later, Liz called to her …nother, "I had a good visit with Phillip and invited him to supper on Wednesday."

"We haven't seen him in a long time," Mama said.

"Not since we went skating the last time. Will he bring Susan with him?" Edie asked, taking loaves of bread out of the oven.

"I didn't think to ask," Liz apologized. "Do you like this, Edie?" She opened the package of cloth she had found for her sister's dress.

"What is it?" Edie asked in wonder. "Are you having two dresses for your wedding?"

Liz hugged her sister and whirled her around the kitchen. "Yes, one for me and one for you."

"I don't wear fancy dresses," Edie protested.

"Oh, but Stephen will want you to on the day you become his sister."

Edie stood still in the middle of the floor. Her face was flushed from working near the stove and then being spun about by her sister. "What do you mean?" she asked in suspicion.

Their mother laughed. "Think about it, Edwina. When Liz marries Stephen Ames, he becomes part of our family. He will be your new brother." She looked up from her chair at Liz.

Liz felt a warm glow to see the pleasure in her mother's face. The lines of pain were not so evident when Mama smiled.

Edie looked thoughtful. "Does Pastor know this?"

"Yes, Dear," her mother said softly.

"Will he mind having someone like me for a sister?" the girl asked seriously.

Liz pulled Edie into a hug. "He already told me he will be happy to have you as his sister."

Edie pulled back and looked up at her sister. "But I haven't been to school, and I walk funny," she whispered.

Liz felt the pressure of tears struggling to surface. "Y
read and write and do arithmetic. I don't think people
notice that you limp a little."

Edie smiled. "I had my own teacher and didn't have to g
to school."

Liz hugged Edie. "I'm glad you chose me to be your teacher."

"Will you please let me go so I can start supper?" Edie said in a voice muffled by her sister's shoulder.

"Will you stand up with me at my wedding?"

Edie giggled and pulled back. "I'll even wear a fancy dress."

❧

The rains came, but the road remained firm enough for Liz to continue to use the buggy. She stopped to have tea with Aunt Sally one soggy afternoon.

"Come in, Child. Been awhile since we've visited."

"How is Fannie? I know you've been spending a lot of time with her," Liz said.

Aunt Sally frowned. "She remains sad. Even when George does cute things, she doesn't smile." Aunt Sally sighed. "I fear she thinks it would be wrong for her to be happy again."

"I'll go call on her. She must know people grieve with her but life has to go on."

"You are going to make a good preacher's wife," Aunt Sally said with a smile. "Now tell me how your mother is feeling."

Liz frowned. "She tries not to show her pain, but I'm sure her back is no better. I asked Phillip about finding someone to come a few days a week to help Edie. I think Mother worries about my sister having to do so much. Mother tries to help, but it's painful for her to stand for any length of time."

"I've been spending so much time with Fannie, I haven't been out to visit. With the roads better, I'll make a point to come out soon." Aunt Sally poured the tea. "Have you seen Meg?"

Liz took a sip from her cup. "No, but Phillip tells me the new doctor is courting her."

Aunt Sally smiled broadly. "I saw David briefly, and he told doctor had asked permission to do so." Taking a sip of ...e put her cup down. "Be a good match. Meg likes to dress ...nd behave like a lady. She can be an asset to the doctor."

I hope you are right," Liz said. "I don't see how keeping a ...ood house and entertaining will help him."

"He looks like he enjoys that sort of thing. I understand he showed up here wearing a fancy suit—on a weekday, no less."

"Yes, I met him that day." She giggled. "And I didn't think anything of it. I thought all doctors dressed like that."

"Maybe they do." Aunt Sally joined in the laughter. "Might make his patients feel better to think he dressed up just to heal them. Anyway, he and Meg will make a good pair. As fast as the town is growing, we need a doctor. If he and Meg want to live in a fancy house and entertain, I'll go to their parties and call the good doctor when I get sick."

Liz put her cup down. "I'm just glad Meg found someone she can be happy with."

"Your mother and I told you the Lord had a plan for that one."

❧

After church on Sunday, Liz was with Mama when she noticed Meg heading straight for them.

"I have someone I'ld like you to meet," she said to Liz's mother.

"I've met the new doctor. He is very nice," Mama answered.

Meg smiled. "I'm glad you like him, but I have another friend I'd like you to meet. May I bring her out to your house?"

Liz looked in wonder from her cousin to her mother. *What is going on here?* She moved closer to her mother.

"You know I'm always at home. Come whenever you can," Mama told her niece.

"Then it's settled," Meg said with a smile. "We will be out later this week."

❧

On Tuesday afternoon when Liz came home from school, she saw another buggy in the yard. Hurrying into the house, she found Meg and another woman sitting at the kitchen table.

"Come meet Hannah," Mama called.

Liz quickly hung up her cloak and turned to greet their guest. A pale, thin girl sat next to Meg. "You are Mary Jenkins's sister," Liz said, taking the girl's hand.

"Yes," came the soft reply. When the girl looked up, Liz saw the same pale blue eyes of her student. "She really talks about you a lot," Hannah continued. "I never got to go to school," she mumbled, dropping her head down again.

Edie joined them at the table. "Hannah says her sister is teaching her to read too," she told Liz. "Now she wants me to teach her to cook."

Liz smiled at her sister's enthusiasm.

Meg put her cup down. "I asked Edie if Hannah could come here a few days a week to help her and to learn to cook."

Liz looked from her mother to her sister. "Edie needs someone to help sometimes. And soon I will be living down the road and not here to do things for her."

Meg smiled. "I'm going to need someone to help me take care of the big house the doctor is talking about building. It would be a help to me if Edie could teach Hannah to cook so she can come and live with me when I get married."

Hannah looked up, and Liz saw the hope in her eyes. "I cook a little bit, but Miss Margaret says her aunt Emily and Edwina are the best cooks in the township. I would be pleased if they could teach me."

Liz saw her cousin's expression. "I had asked your brother if he knew of someone who could help us." She gave Meg a knowing look and turned to Hannah. "You could be an answer to all our prayers."

Mama spoke for the first time. "It sounds to me as if you girls have this all worked out." She reached to take Hannah's hand. "And how will you get to our house, Child?"

"I can walk," the girl said quickly.

"If we put a cot in the kitchen at night, would you like to stay with us for awhile?"

Hannah looked as if she might cry. "I ain't never had a bed to ιeep in. I could use a quilt on the floor."

"No need for that. You go home and talk to your folks and let Miss Margaret know when you want to come here," Mama said gently.

After Meg and Hannah left, Liz helped her mother back to her rocking chair. "Are you sure you want to do this?" she asked, putting a cushion to her mother's back.

"What I want is to put some meat on that child's bones. She is thin as a rail."

"It will be fun to have someone here all day," Edie said gleefully. "I'm getting a new brother and this will be like having a new sister."

"Now we will both be teachers, Edie," Liz told her sister, getting up from her mother's side to help with supper.

"Really?" Edie asked in surprise.

"Of course. I teach at the school and you will teach Hannah how to keep house and cook." She glanced at her mother and smiled. Hannah's presence would keep Mama from pushing herself so hard. One by one, her prayers were being answered.

twenty-two

Liz drove the buggy home from school the next day. She went by way of the new church and smiled in pleasure as Stephen rushed over to help her down.

"I am so happy to see you," he told her with a slight squeeze before he set her on the ground.

"I came to see the progress." She looked at the half-completed building. "It's going up fast."

"Yes." Stephen watched the men on ladders, nailing planks on the framework. "We will celebrate the resurrection of our risen Lord by raising a church in His honor."

"Easter is late this year. Last year Father was still tapping maple trees."

"And next year we will celebrate the event in our own building." He slipped his arm around her waist. Looking down at her, he asked, "Have you been to see Meg? I have been so busy here, I haven't had a chance to stop by."

"Wait till I tell you what she has done." Liz giggled at Stephen's stricken look. "Her latest activities have helped a lot of people."

"What are you saying?"

"Her brother told me she has been going by the Jenkins place. She made friends with the family and has talked Hannah Jenkins into coming to stay with us."

"I heard something about that. Your brother told me you have a new boarder."

"Hannah is not a boarder. She's an answer to prayer. Now the girl has a job, Mother has someone to fatten up, and Edie has a companion."

"Meg managed all that?"

"And she takes time out to charm our new doctor."

"Your cousin has found her place in life. Praise the Lord," Stephen exclaimed.

"It is wonderful to see," Liz agreed and smiled up at him. "Are you coming to supper tonight?"

"I plan to work until dark. Got to get this church built so you and I can have a wedding."

"You're just avoiding us because you know we'll be eating burned biscuits while Hannah learns to cook on a stove instead of a fireplace."

"Matthew tells me work on our house is going well."

"Yes. Father has Ezra and Clyde working full time now. They sleep in the barn, and Edie feeds them."

"I never asked." He grinned. "Can you cook, or am I going to have to sneak down the road to beg meals from my new sister?"

Liz looked scornfully at him until she could no longer hold back a smile. "I can cook. Mother taught me well. And I stopped by Uncle David's store yesterday to find out how soon the cookstove I ordered will be here."

"I'm not sure you should have spent all your savings on a stove. We could have used a fireplace."

"Not with my father around. He'll never build another fireplace. I did ask him to build a brick oven in the yard. They are easier to use than a stove."

"I'm afraid I don't understand all these domestic things."

"Good. You do the preaching, and I'll do the housework. Now I need to get home."

His look of love melted her heart. "Will you come every day?" he pleaded. "I miss seeing you."

"You will see me for the rest of your life," she whispered, climbing back up on the buggy.

Driving through town, Liz heard hammers pounding everywhere. Construction on the academy was in the finishing stages. It would open in the fall. Mr. Howard had invited her to teach there, but she'd refused. It would not be proper for the pastor's wife to work.

Uncle David's brick building was beginning to take shape. She passed a wagonload of bricks going in that direction as she drove home. *He is making it a two-story building. I wonder if he will live upstairs when Meg and Phillip are both married?*

Thoughts of Meg sent Liz's mind scattering in many directions. Her cousin seemed so happy. Liz hardly ever saw her when she was not dressed in a fancy dress with her hair done to perfection. *I could never be like that.* Liz shuddered at the thought. *Good thing the doctor likes seeing Meg looking perfect every day. They will make a good pair.*

Liz arrived home to a house full of laughter. Opening the door, she peeked inside the kitchen. "What is so funny?"

Mama sat rocking in her chair, plying her needle on the dress for Edie. "The girls are having a good time," she said with a smile. "Did you stop by the church?"

Liz walked to her mother's side but managed to look into the parlor on her way. "Yes, but Stephen says he will work until dark and not come for supper." Motioning toward the giggling girls, she asked, "What are they up to?"

"They were going to read to each other, but it sounds as if the lessons you left them got put aside."

"Edie has never had a playmate. I hope this works out."

"Seems to be going just fine. Hannah has had a rough life, but she's finally starting to relax in our home."

"Did you speak to her about church?"

Mama nodded. "She said her folks never went because they didn't have church clothes."

Liz frowned. "I'll have to look around the village and see if others stay away for that reason. The Lord doesn't look at the outside, but unfortunately many people do. I'd better start collecting clothes for people in need so that they will feel comfortable coming to church services."

"You sound like a preacher's wife already," her mother teased.

"I didn't hear you come home," Edie cried, rushing into the kitchen to kiss Liz's cheek.

Liz reached out to hug Edie around the waist, and she smiled at Hannah. "Have you two had fun today?"

Hannah flushed. "I'm supposed to be working."

"We don't work all the time," Mama said. "Why don't you have some milk and cookies now?"

Liz smiled to herself. *Mother will not be happy until she sees Hannah's cheeks filled out and rosy with health.*

"What have you girls cooked up for supper?" she asked.

"I need to go look at the brick oven. We put pans of beans to bake hours ago." Edie hurried out the door with Hannah right at her heels.

Liz looked at her mother. "Are you sure this is not too much for you? I wanted Edie to have help so you would take it easy, but now I'm not so sure it was a good idea."

"You had a fine idea. I like having the two of them chattering away. The first day, I thought Hannah had left her tongue at home. She never said a word." Liz's mother laughed. "But Edie got her livened up in short order."

"I have a skirt you could take in for Hannah. Could you make one of my bodices smaller for her? I'll go get them," Liz said without waiting for an answer.

"While you are in your room, bring down that old homespun dress Edie wears to do the washing. I can make a work dress for Hannah out of it," Mama called after her.

"Will it be long enough?" Liz asked, returning to her mother.

"Won't matter for what I have in mind. I'm going to set the two of them to spring cleaning this house."

Liz groaned. "This house is not dirty," she protested.

"The rugs need to be taken out and beaten, and all the windows washed, and the corners cleaned. We are going to have a wedding this summer, and I want everything to shine."

"Mother, the wedding is at the church, not here." Liz knelt at her mother's side. "You just love to tear up the house every spring."

"That's right. And now you need to get your rug out and work on it."

Liz giggled. "And make it as big as the one Father said y put in your first cabin?"

Mama smiled and stroked her daughter's hair. "Maybe you should concentrate on making a few small rugs to put around the room."

"Father said the kitchen and parlor are all one room."

"Like our first cabin," her mother said dreamily.

"Only I won't have a fireplace. Uncle David says my stove will be here by the time the house is built."

"You can make small rugs to have around that room."

Liz kissed her mother. "I'll go check out the clothes, and then I promise to work on my rug."

"The strips of cloth are sewn together and rolled into balls in the bottom of my clothes press, ready to be crocheted into rugs."

"I will have rugs that smell like lavender," Liz said and scampered up the stairs.

❧

The weather grew hot. Men continued to spend time on the church building. Many of the women in church on Sunday said they were putting in the vegetable gardens so their husbands had more time to give to the building. "We will be in our new church by August," Pastor Ames announced in July.

"Will you take time to come to dinner today?" Liz asked him after services.

"We don't work on the Lord's Day," he said, "so I'd be happy to spend the afternoon with your family—and check on Hannah's progress."

"I baked custard pie, Pastor," Edie told him.

"That's enough to get me to come to dinner." He reached out to greet Hannah. "And how are you today?"

Hannah looked down at her rough hands, "Fine, thank you, Sir."

Pastor took her hands in his. "Will you be at the house today? I look forward to seeing you."

"I'm going to visit my folks this afternoon," she said quietly.

"Will you give them my good wishes, please?"

Liz saw the girl look up with pleasure, "I will do that, Sir."

Meg came up to them on the arm of the good doctor. Both were dressed to the nines. He wore his black suit in spite of the heat, and Meg wore a new hat. "I heard you say you were going to visit your parents, Hannah. Would you like us to give you a ride back to the Millers' house this evening?"

Hannah looked frightened.

"We will be out for a buggy ride and would be happy to pick you up," Dr. Brewster said.

Edie whispered in Hannah's ear, "I'll save you a piece of pie."

Hannah smiled at Edie and then nodded to Meg. "It would be nice of you to give me a ride, Miss Margaret."

❧

It was dusk when the doctor's buggy pulled into the yard at the Millers' farm. Edie bounced out the door to greet them. Hannah jumped down, and the two friends embraced as if they had been separated for several weeks rather than several hours.

Liz stood at the door watching. The doctor helped Meg down, and they walked to the house. "Is Aunt Emily in the kitchen?" Meg asked.

Liz nodded. "And I'm sure Edie could find you a piece of pie."

The doctor smiled. "I've heard about her cooking, so I'm not about to turn down that offer." He looked at the sky. "It'll be light awhile longer. We won't get lost going back." He smiled and followed Meg into the house. "I need to get used to driving on these roads at any time of day or night."

While Liz cut pie and served coffee, she noticed Meg quietly go to her mother's side. When Liz took a cup to Meg, her cousin reached out to her. "I want you to hear this too." Sitting on the stool at Mama's feet, Meg said, "I need your help."

"I thought Mrs. Greely was making your wedding gown," Mama said.

Meg smiled. "Oh, she is. But I need help with Edie."

"Edie?" Liz and her mother said at once.

"I want her to stand up with me, and I know she will refuse if you are not there to coax her." Standing quickly, Meg put her hand on Liz's arm. "I hope you understand why I am asking Edie. She got me to bake cookies and laugh. She helped me see there was a better way to live. I want her by my side when I take my wedding vows."

Liz looked to where Edie and Hannah sat at the table. The men had taken their pie and coffee outside where the evening air was cooler. Then she looked at her mother, who had tears streaming down her face.

"Mama!" She dropped to her mother's side. "Are you all right?"

Mama wiped her cheeks. "I just wish Beth were here. She would be very proud," she said, looking up at her niece. "She was a God-fearing woman and would be overjoyed to see that her daughter is also."

Both Liz and Meg knelt beside her. "She is with us in spirit, Mama," Liz said quietly.

❧

On a bright sunny day in the middle of August, the townspeople crowded into the new church. Even those who did not usually attend came to see the preacher and the schoolmistress take their vows.

Stephen had coaxed Pastor Barnes out of retirement one last time. The old man stood, bent and feeble, at the front of the new building. His voice still rang to the rafters when he spoke. "I married Jonathan and Emily Miller a long time ago. Now I am proud to witness the wedding of their daughter Elizabeth."

Stephen looked at his bride. She stood radiant in her cream-colored dress trimmed in lace. The sun streaks in her blond hair reflected the light filtering through the windows of the church. Next to her stood her petite sister in her first grown-up dress. Edwina had insisted on wearing her hair in her usual style with braids coiled around her head. Nothing could hide the shiny brown color or the strands that had come loose to curl around her face.

At his side, Matthew stood looking uncomfortable in his new shirt. Neither he nor Stephen had worn a suit. They stood in church as they did every week, wearing rough-woven work pants and clean, homespun shirts.

Quietly Stephen took Liz's hand in his and repeated the words Pastor Barnes read. He listened with a swelling heart as Liz proclaimed confidently that she would be his wife until death parted them.

A collective sigh filled the church when Pastor Barnes said, "I now pronounce you man and wife."

As he bent to seal their vows with a kiss, Stephen Ames knew the realization of a dream he had cherished for months and the beginning of dreams that would last a lifetime.